THE COURTLIGHT SERIES

BOOK ONE

SWORN
TO
RAISE

TERAH EDUN

The Courtlight series is a part of the Algardis Universe,

owned by Terah Edun.

Sworn To Raise

Copyright © 2013 by Terah Edun

Distributed through NLA Digital LLC

For information on bulk purchases, please contact the Nelson liaison at

nladigital@nelsonagency.com.

First Edition

Publisher's Cataloging-in-Publication data

Edun, Terah E.

Sworn to raise / by Terah Edun

p.   cm

Summary: When seventeen-year-old peasant girl Ciardis is chosen for a position at court as a companion, she travels across the empire to begin a new life. To survive, she'll need to master intrigue, befriend a crown prince, and learn to control magical abilities she never knew existed.

ISBN 978-1-62051-207-4 (hardcover) • 978-1-62051-186-2 (eBook)

[1. Fantasy. 2. Magic—Fiction. 3. Kings, queens, rulers, etc—Fiction. 4. Courts and Courtiers—Fiction. 5. Love—Fiction.] I. Title.

PZ7.E24963 Sw 2016   [Fic]—d23   2015920433

Reinforced binding

www.terahedun.com

Thank you for your generosity and support.

CHAPTER ONE

Ciardis Vane watched the townspeople jeering as the local Gardis strapped the highwayman into the stocks. Frowning Ciardis wormed her way closer to the front of the crowd, straining to get a peek at the criminal. She felt no pity for the condemned man; he would die tonight, regardless of her feelings. The nightwolves were already pacing, their shadowed forms just visible in the dense tree line, waiting for darkness to fall.

Without the protection of the house wards, the highwayman would be defenseless locked in the stocks. *I wish I could say it will be a quick death,* she thought with clinical detachment, *but they'll probably go for his guts first.* The man deserved no less than death in any case; he had done nothing but steal from—and sometimes kill—those who traveled the Imperial coach roads. "Stand and deliver," indeed!

Ciardis pushed back her heavy brown curls with a sun-bronzed hand. Turning slightly to the side she whispered about his crime with the other washer maids who'd come to see the spectacle. Suddenly, she felt a sharp pinch on her wrist. Turning to see who had interrupted her entertainment, she looked over and frowned down at the younger woman who now stood by her side.

Wringing her hands anxiously, Margaret looked up at Ciardis and gave a quick jerk of her head to the side to indicate they should speak outside the crowd. "You'll want to hear this firsthand, Ciardis," Margaret said with urgency.

"All right, all right," Ciardis muttered as they made their way out of the crowd and down to the washer station with a few other girls trailing behind. The slight blonde woman who scurried next to her was a great source of village gossip, and Ciardis knew that whatever she had to say would be worth leaving the spectacle in the midst of the judge's punishment. To Ciardis, a good piece of gossip was as welcome as spun gold…usually.

When they'd walked far enough from the crowds Margaret was quick to tell Ciardis the news that she'd heard from the weaver's daughter who'd heard it in the apothecary the day before.

Practically bursting with the pent up news Mags bounced on the balls of her feet as she said, "Fervis and the caravan girl…they're *together* Ciardis."

"They're together?" Ciardis said with disgust, "No, he's with me."

Mags shook her whole head, curls bouncing every which way, in denial.

"They were *seen*, getting in a big fight and then…" said Mags.

"So?" interrupted Ciardis in disdain. "That means nothing."

Patiently the girl continued, ignoring the interruption, "And then the girl's father came and threatened to kill Fervis. One thing led to another and now they're bound."

This bit of news hit Ciardis with all the weight of a lead brick.

"Bound?" questioned Ciardis unsteadily. Bound was very different from *together*. Bound meant married, bound meant forever.

Now *she* felt like throwing up.

"Yeah," said Mags softly, "I mean…I thought you'd want to know…first."

At this point Ciardis was staring off in the distance – hand pressed flat against her stomach as if by holding it she could keep her stomach from plummeting in despair.

Minutes later the town bell rang signaling that the highwayman had been sentenced and imprisoned. Everyone would be going back to work now.

Mind numb Ciardis trailed behind Mags, trying to comprehend how her life had just upended.

When she got back to the wash room Ciardis bent over the soapy tub, mind numb as her hands worked mechanically to scrub the red jerkin. Margaret knelt across from her, happily chattering away like a magpie. According to Mags, the miller's son had gotten some passing girl with child. The news had spread like wildfire after the fool had stumbled into the local apothecary's asking for honey's brew. Every woman in town knew that there was only one use for honey's brew, and it wasn't to sweeten tongues.

If the girl had been an orphan, like Ciardis, her swelling belly wouldn't have mattered much. She would have borne the brunt of the town's gossip for the winter months and gone home with a second mouth to feed after the snows melted. But the girl's father was the caravan driver for the only merchant willing to brave the fierce winds of Vaneis in the winter. He'd heard someone's tongue wagging and had confronted the girl before the honey's brew had passed her lips.

Frantic once he'd heard the truth from his daughter's lips, he had gone in search of Fervis Miller. Whatever words had passed between the caravan driver and Fervis over his daughter's 'condition' had been enough to get the message across. Fervis, bruises already darkening on his skin, had shakily gotten down on one knee before five

3

witnesses and asked the girl for her hand in marriage.

The wedding was to take place on the dawn of the Sabbath – just three days hence.

Ciardis frowned contemplating going to their wedding – she would *have* to. Weddings were one of the few forms of entertainment in town, if she didn't go it would definitely take notice. She didn't care. Honestly, she didn't. If that idiot couldn't keep his stick in his pants, then he didn't deserve to wear her ring. Wringing out the last jerkin, she twisted it like she was wringing a stubborn turkey's neck. Or, better yet, Fervis Miller's.

She wiped her hands with a drying cloth, careful to prod Mags for more tidbits at the right intervals. She had finished washing the jerkins and Mags was done with the skirts she was scrubbing. They put them out to dry before the oven fires and then moved on to fold the huge stacks of tunics and pack them in the caravan trunks with dried sprigs of fresh mint. Ciardis thought about the stolen moments she'd had with the miller's son. In the summer, they'd picnicked in the meadows, and throughout mid-winter he'd held her waist as they flew across the ice of the secluded mountain ponds. Memories of the soft touches exchanged and the ardor in his voice when he'd promised that he'd petition for her vows were still imprinted upon her mind. He'd promised over and over that he'd convince his mother somehow that Ciardis, orphan girl with skin the color of pale pecans and unruly chestnut curls, was the young woman that should be her daughter-in-law.

Ha! Last spring, she and Fervis had even hatched a plan for her to bump into his mother as she left morning prayers at the church. They'd painstakingly played out the scene while laying on fresh hay in the cobbler's barn. When the day to bump into his mother had come Ciardis had tried to strike up a conversation. But from the moment the conversation began, it was clear from the rancor in the woman's tone and the disparaging look in her eyes that she considered her son's marriage prospects far above the town's orphaned girl.

Guess she was right, Ciardis thought with irony, *He's going to get a caravan merchant's daughter who lifts her skirts for the first young man she sees instead.*

Frustrated and tired, Ciardis threw her basket of clothes down on the floor with such force that she startled Margaret right out of her monologue. "What's with you?" Mags asked, dark eyes wide.

"Nothing, nothing," muttered Ciardis. "There was a ground bug on the floor—just wanted to get it before it escaped."

Inside she was seething, calling Fervis every dirty name she knew. She'd wasted two whole years on that idiot. Two years of listening to his constant whining about grain prices and the boring bakery gossip in his uncle's shop.

She'd set her sights on him at age fifteen. He had been boring then, and he was boring now, but she could live with boring. What she *couldn't* live with were the pangs of hunger after an evening with no meals, a month without meat, or the backbreaking work of being a temporary field hand. With a man like Fervis, set with a steady income from being in a miller's family, Ciardis could have a life of leisure…or close to it. But now thanks to that lout she was ruined. Here she was, seventeen with no nest egg or dowry to buy a husband, and she'd already snubbed every boy within twenty miles to show Fervis her devotion. Her devotion, for crying out loud! Fat lot of good it did her now.

After finishing the last load of laundry, she eased out of the hot sauna room and into the outer chamber where Sarah, the dour head cleaner and accountant, kept the tally chips. The tally chips were small marks color coded for a task. A red chip for hard to clean garments like the red leather jerkins, a blue chip for folding a basket, a green chip for pressing and ironing. She counted hers as she walked down the hallway to Sarah's office. Today she'd washed three loads by hand and pressed and packed a further two. That was just enough to get her a decent tally at the end of two weeks' work. She had to pay the innkeeper soon.

Handing the chips over to Sarah, she waited impatiently in front of the scarred wooden desk. The woman took forever with anything, particularly when that anything involved money. She squeezed the last shilling out of every washing cloth and piece of soap she bought.

At last, Sarah handed over her payment and she went home. She even had a few extra coins, enough for a small bowl of soup with bread—*huzzah!* Since she could pay in cash she didn't have to worry about adding tonight's dinner to her tab, then. The innkeeper was a pleasant man, but he always charged interest to the month's tab when she did that.

She was freezing by the time she stepped into the warm inn kitchen, even though she was bundled in three layers, with woolen pants on under her skirts. Rushing to the fire, she warmed her chafed hands over the flames.

Out of the corner of her eye she saw the only male waiter for the inn rush in through the swinging panel doors from the tavern. From the noise that wafted in behind Kelly the place was packed with journeymen. *Must be that caravan that's on its way out,* she thought as she nibbled on a cracker she'd filched from a side table on her way into the kitchen.

Kelly began to hurry out just as fast carrying a platter filled with hot mutton and an empty kettle which swung erratically from his hand. She ducked to dodge the errant kettle and said irritably, "Watch where you're going, Kelly, you big lout! You almost brained me." Ciardis pushed her scarf back off her silky mane as she straightened up, scowling.

"Sorry, lass," Kelly said, already rushing through the swinging panels and into the tavern. Noise flooded through the open doorway. *Must be a large crowd tonight*, Ciardis mused.

"Hey, lass!" said the rotund cook, "Good to see you." He leaned close, smelling heavily of savory spices, and said in a low voice, "Mind your way when you head back to your room, hear? Lots of knights about, and not all of 'em Gardis, if you catch my meaning."

She caught his meaning, all right. "Thanks for the warning," she said gravely. Grabbing two pieces of fresh baked bread and a bowl for soup, she had the tavern maid dish out the soup under the watchful eye of the cook. Paying for the meal she grabbed a spoon and left the kitchen.

She decided to take the back stairs with her lentil soup and bread. She navigated the creaky flight with her satchel digging into her back, balancing her plate in both hands. She ate as soon as she'd opened the door, ducked into the stuffy darkness of her room, and then eased down on the lumpy bed.

Ciardis went to sleep not long afterward, still furious about the miller's son, but a tiny twinge of self-doubt also fluttering in her belly.

At half past midnight, a sound broke through Ciardis's dreams and sent her lurching out of bed. She'd heard the light creak of the stairs outside her door. Frowning, she threw off the heavy covers and grabbed the knife she'd hidden between the mattress and wall. *Must be a drunken soldier.*

Her room was barely big enough to stand in, with a sloped ceiling and a mattress that took up most of the floor. If a soldier cornered her in here, there was no way she'd be able to fight back...except for the six inches of steel blade in her hand. Best to avoid the situation altogether. Thinking of her options she knew the roof washer was her only bet. It'd be tricky to maneuver to get up there while holding something but Ciardis quickly decided that she'd rather have the knife in her hand than in her belt. She quickly grabbed the rickety stool in the corner and pushed off the accumulated clothes to the floor. Standing on it with the knife in her right hand, she reached up and pushed at a panel in the ceiling, easing it up and placing it next to the opening. She gripped the edge of the ceiling with both hands and swung herself up and over, then slipped the panel back into place. Now she stood in the small crawl space between the room and the roof. It was insulated as well as it could be but the ceiling still leaked warmth in deep winter. Even with the leak, at times like this, she was glad she'd never gotten the panel fixed. It made her claustrophobic to think of being stuck in that little closet of a room with no fresh air. Careful to move silently she grabbed the tarp that latched over a hole in the roof that had never been fixed and eased out the nails that held it in place. Leaving the ceiling panel loose and tarp in place had numerous downsides…but in this case the advantage of escaping her room more than outweighed them.

As soon as she wiggled through the small opening, the bitterly cold wind chilled her to the bone, even though she was still dressed in layers. Her fingers began to feel numb. Trying to evade the chill she hastily rearranged the tarp and fisted her hands in order to pull back her trailing fingers as far as she could into her sleeves. Unfortunately that wasn't going to work for very long. She'd need to use her hands at some point.

It must be close to the freezing point, she thought while her teeth chattered. Her little room had a heat spell on it to ward off the worst of the cold, but out here she'd freeze to death if she wasn't careful. She couldn't hear anyone in the hallway now, but that meant nothing. Making a quick decision, she headed across the roof toward the stables. It wasn't the best place to sleep, but it was better than being raped, and Robe would look after her there.

The steep roof had peaks that rose up into the night sky and furrows that dipped sharply to help the accumulated snow slide off more quickly. That also meant there were a lot of snowdrifts at the wall base and, even worse, ice. She cursed under her breath as she struggled to maintain her footing. She saw the irony in escaping a drunken soldier only to bash her brains out on the ice below.

Upon reaching the roof's far edge, she carefully descended an ice-slick ladder to the walkway that connected the inn's second floor to the barn's upper level, where they kept the pegasus stalls. Hurrying now, she soon reached the welcome warmth of the stables. As soon as she stepped inside, the straw dust hit her allergy-sensitive nose and made her sneeze. Those allergies, especially in the spring with the dust and dandruff, were a dangerous combination. Consequentially, at any time of year, but particularly in high pollen season, the stables represented her refuge of last resort.

Ignoring her discomfort for the moment, she headed for the opposite end of the row of stalls, where the stable manager's quarters lay. That was where Robe lived. He was a man twice her age, but with the mind of someone much younger. He loved animals, and they loved him. She shook her head silently, shivering. It was a simple-minded mentality but worked well for Robe and the stable owner. Garth had decided that a man with half the intellect of the others and a childlike enjoyment of the animals would be less likely to run off. He'd given Robe a home at the stables, steady meals and a few coins once a month for his services in training and caring for the pegasi. In Robe's eyes it was a good trade: his skills in the stable for a home. In Ciardis's view he'd been robbed of a proper income. But at the same time, she'd hate to think of what might happen to him on the streets.

Easing the door open, she sidled into the office area, which Robe used as his "pretty things" room. It was half-filled with rocks he'd picked up, shirts he refused to wear but loved to look at, and bright scraps of cloth pinned to the walls. Sometimes he kept colicky foals in here, too. Once he'd kept a baby snow leopard for a month—even built a nest for it. How Robe had managed to catch the dangerous creature, even a baby snow leopard had claws that rivaled the knife in her hand, and convinced the pegasi to keep his secret she would never know, but once Garth, the innkeeper, found out about the cub, all hell broke loose. It had taken some convincing, but Robe had handed the cub over to the innkeeper. Garth had told Robe he was sending it to a sanctuary, but really the innkeeper had sold it to a noble idiot who liked to keep dangerous pets.

Ciardis went over to the wall nook where Robe kept a couch. Carefully putting aside a pile of brightly colored shirts, she slid down onto the couch and curled up for an uneventful night's rest. She woke to find a bowl of cooling porridge on the floor near her dangling arm and pale sunlight shining down on her face from the narrow window. With a wry smile, she reached for the mashed mix of raisins, milk, and oats. She was pretty sure it was the same thing the pegasi ate. Only Robe would give this to a person and consider it a proper meal for a human.

After eating and visiting the bathhouse, she headed out for another day of drudgery at the washer station. Occasionally she would pull her arm over her head and the muscles along her shoulder to stretch her arm as she walked. When she arrived, she saw a lady with stylishly pale hair standing inside Sarah's office, arguing with the old washerwoman. Ciardis stopped in the hallway and listened to the conversation. The woman was shaking a knight's long coat in her hand. It was a beautifully vibrant red color – like the plumage of a dusk hen in spring. Ciardis also knew it was soft as butter because she'd handled ten jerkins of similar make yesterday afternoon. Listening to the conversation she heard the woman demand, "What will it take? Twenty shillings? Forty?"

What will what take? Ciardis wondered with wide eyes. Whatever it was, this woman was offering two months' salary for it.

Sarah shook her head slowly. "No. Ya can't have my recipe."

Recipe? What are they talking about? Realizing what it would look like if they caught her loitering in the hall, she contrived to look busy by shifting around and sorting the piles of clothes stacked against the far wall. Mags appeared out of nowhere with a curious look on her face, but Ciardis quickly waved her away from the pile of clothes she was sorting. She didn't want to finish before the conversation in Sarah's office was over. Mags walked away in a huff.

"Really, woman," came the exasperated lady's reply from Sarah's office. "I just need it for the red costumes. Is it really so costly for you?"

Furiously thinking, the pieces to the puzzle clicked together for Ciardis. *Red was a princely dye*, one of the few that took skill to harvest and prepare. Ciardis was known across the Vale for her red dye which she made from a combination of mountain plants and one elusive ingredient that Sarah had been trying to drag out of her for years. Ciardis refused to give up her secret ingredient, Mountain Moon Leaf, and Sarah hadn't been able to devise a substitute. More than anything Sarah loved her money and she knew that as long as she had access to Ciardis's dye she could charge a hefty fee to individuals interested in getting their garments cleaned in a way that wouldn't harm the bright red fabrics, which was why Ciardis had been in charge of all the red jerkins yesterday.

Sarah had warned her not to let the colors run, but quite frankly, she knew Ciardis's cleaning mixtures were the best. Sarah was just lucky that Ciardis couldn't venture out into her own laundry business; the Vale customer base wasn't big enough for more than one.

"That old harpy," Ciardis muttered after listening to the conversation. Sarah was trying to sell *her* dye for quite a bit of money and Ciardis was quite sure Sarah had no intention of sharing in the profits either.

As the pale-haired lady stalked out, Ciardis hurried out the side door and around to the front of the building to catch up with her. "Ma'am! Ma'am!" called Ciardis. When the lady stopped, she rushed up to her and blurted, "If it's the mix for the red you want, I can sell it to you."

"My, what a pretty thing you are," said the lady as she eyed the girl. She reached forward to touch the loose strands of hair that had escaped from Ciardis's bun. She looked curiously at the girl's bronze skin and almond-shaped golden eyes. "How…unique," she said. "Now, what was it you were saying?"

"The mix," said Ciardis softly. "The soap mix, ma'am. It's *my* recipe." She raised her chin firmly and said, "It's yours for thirty-five shillings."

The lady's dark brown eyes flashed in amusement as they met Ciardis's golden ones. Ciardis grimaced, but held her ground, the woman probably knew Ciardis couldn't make more than fifteen shillings in a month, twenty if she were lucky. "Well," the lady said slowly, "I suppose I could agree to that. Bring the mix to my room this evening. I'm staying at the Green Inn."

Nodding, Ciardis backed away respectfully. She was already late for her day's work. Whirling around she ran down the hallway to the back of the building to the washer station to start her tasks. She'd been lucky that Sarah hadn't come outside while they were talking.

Hours later while fixing the lye for the next morning's batches, she overheard a bunch of the other girls talking about the mysterious guest from the South. Ciardis carried the large wooden tub filled with the ingredients for the lye outside. Mixing it there was always preferable, even in the cold. The stench would have been horrible in the little mixing room.

Lugging it outside she went to the area just behind the steam room filled with charcoal burners. Setting the heavy tub down with a heavy *thud*, she reached for the solution strapped to her in a round gourd. As she stirred it in a clockwise motion the voices drifted over.

Their conversation was just high enough for Ciardis to overhear from the other side of the steam room while the wall between them hid her from view.

"Did you see her?" one said in an excited whisper that Ciardis thought was Marianne, the candle maker's daughter.

"She has to be a—" said another voice, but Ciardis couldn't hear the last word.

Has to be a what? She pushed her ear against the wall in frustration, trying to catch as much of the conversation as possible.

A third girl, Rosie, squealed, "Oh my Lord. It's not possible. Why would one of *those* people come here? It's unheard of for them to come so far out—we're practically in the middle of nowhere, and at the very edge of the Algardis Empire."

"Who knows," sniffed Marianne with disdain, "But *I* won't be having anything to do with her. You know what they say: anything goes in Sandrin. I mean, those type of people are abominations. Companions – they're nothing but women with loose morals."

"Of course; I wouldn't either," Rosie stammered. "I just meant that it's exciting to see one so far from Court."

The second voice chimed in derisively, but Ciardis couldn't make out the words. Ciardis recognized the voice as belonging to Amanda. After a moment, the girls rounded the corner and saw Ciardis bent over the mixing basin. When Amanda saw Ciardis, she raised an eyebrow and quickly shushed her companions, "Hush, both of you."

The three town girls gave Ciardis ice-cold smiles, polite but distant while their eyes flitted over her faded dress, which had large spots where the color had faded away.

She returned their greeting and turned away, knowing that they had nothing to share with her. Even though she put on a brave face, she was wishing all the while that she had the courage to ask about the strange woman in their small vale. She wondered who the woman was, where she was from – could it really be Sandrin, and why she was here in Vaneis.

That evening, Ciardis gathered her last pound of precious mix for cleaning red dyed cloth and leathers. Carefully weighing it she put it on a small scale and used a stone weight as a countermeasure. One pound exactly. Satisfied Ciardis headed for the Green Inn. There were three inns in town – the one Ciardis stayed in which doubled as a pegasi way station, and another which was a rundown shack with two rooms managed by an old crone and her son. The third inn, the Green Inn, was the one that the rich guests, like the caravan leader, always used. Looking around the main tavern Ciardis made a beeline for Mary after realizing she had no idea where the lady was staying. Mary was the head waitress and one of the few people whom she considered a friend. Tonight was busy – Mary had to continuously jump up to grab the beer and meals ordered by the men cramming the room. After a few quick words and directions from Mary who remembered the woman from her first day at the inn, Ciardis headed up to Room Three on the bottom floor. She knocked firmly on the door.

It hadn't even been latched. It eased open with a creak.

CHAPTER TWO

Absentmindedly, Ciardis noted that the creak on the door could be fixed with a little oil to loosen the stiff hinges at the base. She'd tell Mary later.

The white-haired woman stood near the window, staring at a piece of parchment—a letter. *She can read,* Ciardis noted enviously. She had always wanted to be able to, but couldn't afford to pay for the schoolmarm's private lessons, and as an orphan, the local villagers who paid the schoolmarm's yearly wages for the biweekly classes wouldn't let her attend.

The woman raised an elegant hand and gestured for Ciardis to come in. "I'm so glad you came," said the woman. "This mix will do wonders for my costumes."

"Costumes?" asked Ciardis.

"Yes," said the woman with a laugh. "You didn't think they were battle garb or something, did you?" Blushing, Ciardis kept silent. That was exactly what she had thought. Military uniforms were often red to hide bloodstains.

The woman stepped forward, her dress swishing on the polished wooden floors. Pressing her finger to her lips she looked at Ciardis with studied nonchalance as she eyed her up and down. It made Ciardis feel like a bug under a farsight lens and she struggled not to squirm under the attention. Ciardis held up the red mix, hoping to bring the woman's attention back to the reason she'd come.

Taking it deftly, the woman said, "Have you always been a laundress?"

"Yes," said Ciardis. "As long as I can remember."

"Nothing else?" asked the woman.

"No," replied Ciardis, a bit resentfully. Heavens, she'd been lucky to get *this* job. No one wanted to hire a girl with no family ties.

Coyly the woman tilted her head, showing off her smooth neck and beautifully draped curls in a practiced look, "And is that all you've ever wanted to be?"

"Of course not," Ciardis snapped. "But there aren't many jobs open to an orphaned girl, now are there?"

The woman's eyes flashed as she laughed and said, "Ah, so you *do* have some fire in you!"

This time, Ciardis met her eyes dead on and said, "If you'll pay me what was promised then our agreement will be done, milady. I should be getting back to my quarters."

"How would you like to do what I do?" the woman asked.

"Seeing as I have no idea what it is you do, milady, that would be hard to know."

"My dear," the woman responded grandly, "I am a companion."

Ciardis blanched and almost fell down as she scrambled to lower herself into a curtsy. She cursed inwardly at herself for her awkwardness. "M-my apologies, milady. I-I didn't know. I expected…I mean, I didn't know what a companion looked like."

As Ciardis raised her eyes, she noted that the woman was looking at her curiously. "Yes, well, we don't always go around advertising ourselves," she finally responded. "You may call me Lady Serena."

Ciardis closed her eyes briefly and nodded. Her thoughts were whirling excitedly inside her head. *A companion...a real companion?*

Companions were legendary fixtures of the Emperor's court. Stories were told of their beauty, their grace and above all their power. All of the best noble houses had one on staff...at least, that's what she'd heard.

Straining to remember the girls' conversation about the visitor from the South, Ciardis recalled Marianne's whisper from earlier that day: *"You know what they say: anything goes in Sandrin. I mean, those type of people are abominations. Companions – they're nothing but women with loose morals."*

But it couldn't be. It was impossible—companions never left the courts, and she had no markings. *I'll sell her the product and go,* Ciardis thought.

Aloud, she said, "My apologies, Lady Serena. I—we—don't get many companions so far from court."

Laughing, the woman told her, "You'll have to learn to control your vocal inflections better, dear. You've told me so much while speaking so very little! You don't believe me, do you?" Before Ciardis could protest, Lady Serena pulled her lapel down to show her the mark of a true member of the Companions' Guild.

Just below her collar bone was the emblem of Imperial courts – a red lion rampant, encircled by the twisted vines of the Companions' Guild's symbol.

Ciardis's eyes widened. There could be no mistaking that mark. The woman was as she claimed. Looking into her eyes, Ciardis whispered, "Did you mean it? When you asked if I wanted to be a companion?"

The woman nodded with a sly smile. "You have the build, and, shall we say, an *exotic* look. I can't imagine you wouldn't be able to find a suitable patron."

When she heard that, Ciardis felt faint.

Before she could react, Lady Serena said, "Think about it carefully, Miss...?" She looked at Ciardis expectantly.

"Ciardis," the orphan girl blurted out.

"Ah, even your name is lovely. You won't have to change that." Lady Serena looked around to make sure no one was within earshot, then leaned toward Ciardis and said, "My birth name was Gertrude."

Ciardis stifled a giggle as the lady straightened and smiled. "Ah, a sense of humor—good. You'll need it. I'll sponsor you, young Ciardis, but it's a hard life. Yet, it is worth every deprivation if you find the right patron." Regally she tossed her hair as she continued, "We leave with the caravan in the morning, Ciardis. Say your goodbyes before then."

Nodding mutely, Ciardis turned in a daze to leave the room. "My dear?" came Lady Serena's melodic voice. Ciardis turned back. Lady Serena held a small coin bag out to her. "Your thirty-five shillings."

It wasn't until Ciardis was out of the inn that she realized that Lady Serena had never considered that Ciardis might refuse her offer.

When she closed the door and leaned back against it, she realized her palms were wet from nervous perspiration. She wiped her sweaty hands on the fabric at her waist, and pocketed the money, thinking with envy, *I doubt very much that anyone ever says no to her.*

***

That evening, Ciardis sat quietly in her room. She looked around in the flickering lamplight, taking in the bare walls, the threadbare clothes hanging on pegs, the rag-filled mattress.

She had nothing tying her to Vaneis. Her parents were long dead. Fervis Miller was a fool, and Sarah had no intention of ever promoting her, no matter how often she demonstrated her worth. The best friends she had were Mags, who was flighty, and Robe, who would scarcely notice she was gone. No family, no lasting friendships and no lands were holding her here in this provincial backwater town.

"How hard a life could it be, living as a pampered companion?" Ciardis said to herself as she went around the room and picked up the few items that littered the floor, eyeing their weight and worth.

A scarf thrown carelessly on the bed had been a gift from a kindly old woman. A book about a lady knight with purple eyes and a passion for justice—one of her few treasured possessions—lay near the window. So far she'd paid Amanda at the Green Inn twice to read it to her. It was that precious.

With her mind made up to leave Vaneis, she packed the three dresses she owned, the scarf, the book, some herbs for soap mix, and thirty shillings for the road in her satchel.

The next morning, she made sure to pay the innkeeper five shillings for her month's rent. She filled a small rucksack full of food for her journey and left the inn with a smile on her face.

Once outside, Ciardis squinted, looking up and down the caravan line. There were six wagons attached to huraks – large, ponderous beasts that looked like oxen with claws. The huraks were all clearly anxious to go as they snorted and pawed the fresh snow with the three dagger-shaped claws on each foot.

You and me both, friend. She clutched her two cloth bags and stared around for Lady Serena, trying not to seem too obvious.

"All riders up!" rang the call down the line. Ciardis gave up her nonchalant look in favor of panic and began to search frantically. She didn't see Lady Serena anywhere. What if it had all been a cruel joke? After one last look, shoulders slumped, she turned to leave.

And then she heard a familiar voice call out, "My dear! My dear Ciardis! Here I am—over here!"

Ciardis turned and raised her hand to shield her eyes as she squinted into the morning sun. Lady Serena sat in the third carriage from the front in the long line, waving a handkerchief out the window.

"Hey, you!" said a loud baritone voice. It was the caravan driver on the front wagon. He was looking at Ciardis as he stood on the driver's bench. "In or out?" he bellowed.

Ciardis hurried to obey his command, jumping up into the lady's carriage. It abruptly lurched forward, and she fell onto her hands and knees. Lady Serena's laughter echoed in the close interior. "My dear," she said lightly as she reached down to pull Ciardis up by her hand, "We have *so* much to work on."

Ciardis settled in on the bench across from her and watched as the snowy, forested vale went by. The carriage glided across the packed snow on huge steel blades. Occasionally she glanced over at Lady Serena who, true to her name, was serene and composed as she sat reading a small book.

Ciardis was careful to keep her face turned towards the window while she secretly wiped a tear from her left eye. Firmly reminding herself of her great luck, Ciardis was determined to think of this as an adventure…a grand new life even. She was happy to get away from a dead end life in a village that was too small. *But maybe,* whispered some little corner of her mind, *just maybe, I'll miss that village. After all, it's the only home I've ever known. Will they even like me in the city? Will I be the country fool – pitied by the other trainees?*

Lady Serena's voice startled her out of her thoughts. "Now, first things first. What is your full name?"

"Ciardis Rafaela Vane, Lady Serena," Ciardis replied.

"Vane, Vaneis. A very similar variation – most likely truncated." the older woman said thoughtfully. "So you were named for your place of birth?"

"Yes, mistress, I suppose I was."

"And your heritage?" asked Serena.

Ciardis looked closely at the lady to see if she was mocking her. As an afterthought, Lady Serena added, "You can call me Serena in private."

At last, Ciardis replied, simply, "Orphan."

"Yes, yes, I know that," came Serena's exasperated reply, "but what about your parents' backgrounds?"

Ciardis shrugged. "I didn't know my father, and my mother died when I was two. She was a dirty wayfarer – at least that's what the townsfolk said. The baker said she moved from place to place, never staying in one area too long. I went to live with a local family that didn't have children but once they started birthing their own kids they decided they didn't need another mouth to feed. The mother and father, the Kiltrens, sent me to the washer station until I was old enough to have a room of my own at the inn."

"Hmm. Well, with a last name like Vane, you're probably baseborn. Rather unique eyes though, perhaps a mother with a wild heritage. The isles are full of humans with exotic eyes like yours," said Lady Serena without a hint of regret. The carriage shook as it struggled over the harsh and bumpy terrain, tossing them about. Once the carriage shook so badly that the tilted angle sent Ciardis and Serena flying into the side of the carriage wall. By the time they had righted themselves, Ciardis had stifled her anger and gotten her face under control.

Nothing Serena had said was untrue or anything she hadn't heard before. Taunts from village children could be cruel. "Little bastard baseborn," they used to call her. Sometimes they would even change their schoolyard rhymes to mock her when she passed, staggering under the loads of laundry for the day. Once she was alone and away from prying eyes she had cried herself to sleep almost every night.

The barbs had hurt then, and the words still hurt now.

Eyeing her, Lady Serena said, "Happens to the best of us." Before Ciardis could digest that, she continued, "Look, Ciardis, being a companion is about more than mastering the art of the instrument, the tone of your voice, and the pleasure of your presence – visually or otherwise. Companions are more than jewels on a patron's arm…they are *useful*. All companions perform services for their Patrons. For instance, I am a projecting companion. Projecting is my magical talent. Anything my Patron, Lord Cannon, wishes to see, whether practical or whimsical, I can bring forth."

Serena opened her palm. Slowly a bright blue energy began to build – swirling up from the lines in her hand to become a miniature blue tornado of light the size of a kitten. It solidified quickly after forming into the image of a miniature form of Serena in full color and wearing a beautiful dress. The miniature began to waltz in the palm of Lady Serena's hand while Ciardis watched in delight. Serena said, "I can make this any size I want." She waved her hand at the bench, and suddenly the miniature jumped from its place on her palm and there was a full-sized version sitting primly next to Ciardis in the next second.

The full-sized vision of Serena winked at Ciardis and then dissipated just as quickly as it had appeared. Proudly Serena said, "I am also ranked as a Master Tactician. You can't become a military officer through magic alone, but because of my memorization skills and ability to project training modules, I have excelled at training Lord Cannon's soldiers in military tactics."

"But…but I don't *have* any magic," Ciardis said shamefully.

"Yes, and that will make your life more difficult," Serena said bluntly. "There are companions with no magic, but their mundane skills are without peer. Kira, the assassin companion, is so skilled in the art of the knife that she has killed three princes at the request of her lord. And Miranda, the artist companion, builds automatons so lifelike that they're used to attract customers in all the shops of her lady's business ventures."

As Ciardis shifted uncomfortably, Lady Serena said, "Now what can you do for us?" As Ciardis opened her mouth to reply, Serena cut her off with a wave of her hand. "And do not mention soaps."

It was going to be a long ride to the courts of Sandrin.

CHAPTER THREE

In fact it took six agonizing days to reach Lineaus, the way station outside the capital city. Sandrin sat on a bright bay of the same name, a sparkling port city guarded by the Lords of the Windswept Isles.

As they walked around the town, Lady Serena pointed to places they could go for what she called Ciardis's "wardrobe intervention." "In that building there," she said while pointing out the red structure with beautiful inlaid glass on their right, "is the place with the best mud facial this side of the Ameles Forest." Ciardis glanced quickly at the shop front as they passed. "And this dress shop," said Serena, "is where we'll get some attire to make you look appropriate for an appearance before the Guild Council. We can't have you looking like a ragamuffin, now can we?"

Ciardis tugged anxiously at the heavy brown overskirt that she wore. It was true that what she was wearing was rather threadbare...and ugly. She voiced her only concern, though. "Milady, I don't have the coin for the likes of this."

"Oh heavens, dear," said Serena, "I know you don't. As your

sponsor in this venture, I will provide for your lodging and attire. At least until you have been reviewed by the Companions' Guild for potential trainee status."

Over the next several hours, Ciardis was prodded and measured.

When Serena asked, "Are your undergarments linen or silk?" Ciardis gave her a look like a deer facing the glow of a bright lantern in the dark forest. She didn't want to answer because she wasn't wearing any aside from the woolen pants she wore to keep her legs warm under the skirt.

Reading her expression, Serena tersely ordered five pairs from the salon owner and snippily informed Ciardis that she would be enrolled in an intense class on "personal hygiene maintenance," whatever that was, as soon as she had settled in as a trainee.

The measurements continued while Serena sipped tea and ate biscuits contently in the corner. Occasionally, Serena would interrupt the silence with lightning fast decisions on the cut of cloth and fit of the dresses Ciardis was trying on. Eventually Serena began to confer with the salon assistant on the best fabric and dyes to compliment what she referred to as Ciardis's "decidedly brownish" hair.

"Tell me, Ciardis," Serena said over the shop assistant's head, "Your skin is chafed—I assume due to your duties and the cold temperatures of a winter in the vale. But what's your skin like in the summer?"

Relieved to hear a question that she could answer, Ciardis hurriedly said, "Quite tough, ma'am. At least, compared to those in the vale. I even got calluses when I wrung out the clothes in the river."

Serena grimaced. That was not the answer she had been looking for.

Serena tapped her fan in irritation. "This could complicate your debut."

Turning to the shopkeeper, she explained, "We'll stick with the current attire, including long sleeves to mask the rough patches on her skin. I'll send orders for more garments in the spring after we've started her on a strict moisturizing regimen."

He nodded in acknowledgement from the counter where he was tallying up the cost of all the gowns Serena was purchasing. The shopkeeper's assistant never raised her head from where she was focused at Ciardis's waist stitching a small piece of gold cloth with a flower design to improve the overall look.

Serena continued, "And if the Council of the Companions' Guild judge you worthy as a companion trainee, as they surely will, all your needs will be seen to before the Patron Hunt."

"Patron Hunt?" asked Ciardis, feeling a bit dazed at everything, as the sour-faced shopkeeper's assistant held up the third swatch of dark blue up against her skin in as many seconds. The assistant looked to Serena and the shopkeeper for the decision. Ciardis had learned a few dresses back to not even bother voicing her desires in this venture. It never ended well.

Serena indicated her approval with a subtle nod. "Yes, this color made into a simple frock will do nicely." She turned to the shopkeeper and said, "Oh, she'll also need a few accessories—scarves, pins, and a cloak, as well as some light weaver's dresses for her tutorials."

"Aye, milady."

Serena turned her attention back to Ciardis. "Now, where were we? Ah, yes. In three months' time, you will be presented at the Patron Hunt, a gala that lasts for two days and three nights. At the end, you must be claimed by a Patron."

Ciardis bit her lip and nodded as if she understood, though she really didn't understand anything at all. They left with three packs of dresses wrapped in paper and a promise from the shopkeeper that the rest would make its way to the Companions' Guild before two nights had passed.

Once they got settled in the carriage, they proceeded eastwards, toward the ocean. Soon, Ciardis could hear the squawk of water birds as they flew along the quays, their wings outspread. She wondered if she might catch a glimpse of the Imperial palace. Surely it was grand enough to be seen from atop the gates.

They rounded a bend, and there it was: a huge, sprawling palace of sparkling pink marble blocks, spires, and turrets, stretching as far as Ciardis could see. She giggled nervously as her gaze looked over the castle and then she took a moment to look at the white beach with beautiful turquoise waters that lay off to her right.

Ciardis was startled out of her exploration at the sharp poke of Serena's finger on her shoulder. She admonished Ciardis, "Do not *ever* let me hear that noise coming out of your mouth again." She shuddered delicately. "Companions do not giggle."

"Yes, milady," Ciardis whispered.

Their carriage pulled up to the gates and entered a wide courtyard decorated with fountains spraying water from spouts every which way. The manicured lawn spread before her with elaborately shaped trees and green grass that would leave farmers with envy back home. As it eased to a halt, Serena said grandly, "Welcome, my dear, to the Companions' Guild."

They stepped out into the courtyard, and Ciardis reveled in the smell of fresh salt air. "This is not an Imperial palace?" she inquired after a long moment.

Serena responded negatively. "Well, don't dawdle," she soon called out as she began to rush into the cavernous entryway. Ciardis was almost left behind, and she hurried to grab their purchases from the top of the steerage.

"Of course I can see why you might mistake it for an Imperial palace," Serena said when Ciardis had caught up, and for a second, the girl had no idea what she meant. Then she continued, "This castle was built decades ago for Queen Margie, you see. She was the first companion—and only companion, thus far—to rise to Imperial Consort. The Queen bequeathed the castle and a tidy sum of money to a group of wealthy companions after she passed to the heavens, for the training and establishment of a guild—" She broke off.

"Sarah!" squealed Serena as she stared up the stairs to a woman perched at a desk on the balcony a story above. The woman stood up abruptly and looked over the staircase railing next to her at Serena's cry. Serena rushed up a small staircase to the imposing white desk which stood parallel to it. Sarah, the bespectacled woman with blue-streaked hair piled on top of her head, came out from behind the desk she attended to greet Serena. Ciardis took in the scene with a little smirk, thinking, *companions don't giggle…and yet they can squeal?*

Serena, noticing that Ciardis was again lagging behind, motioned for her to join them. "Sarah, may I present the Companions' Guild's newest recruit: Ciardis Vane."

Sarah's lips curled in amusement as she took in Ciardis, who was lugging multiple packages and her belongings from Vaneis up the winding stairs. "Wayfarer stock, I see," Sarah murmured, then leaned forward to whisper into Serena's ear, "And she's just *barely* the newest recruit. Another recruit checked in just hours before – although Ciardis can of course take the title for now." The blue-haired woman leaned back with a smug look.

Serena's gasp was audible from where Ciardis stood on the landing. Ciardis could barely hear them and she had no idea what the gasp was about. Sarah continued with a sarcastic roll of her eyes because she hated Vana just as much as Serena did, "Our *beloved* Lady Vana rolled in this morning with a Chimaeran girl!"

"What!" Serena said, shocked. "Chimaeran? Impossible!" She was clearly distressed.

"It's true!" Sarah hastily explained, "She was apparently just passing by the Summer Isles and happened upon this young girl."

"She was 'just passing by' the Summer Isles?" echoed Serena. She then said something quite unladylike. "No one *just* '*passes by*' the Summer Isles. The number of pirates in that region alone requires an armed escort of at least three destroyers to ward them off!" Serena paced in front of the desk. "That…that…*harridan* did this just to spite me! I know she did!"

Ciardis looked at her askance as Serena had basically just questioned the woman's heritage…all for what?

"Oh, dear, hush now. You're frightening the new recruit," Sarah said soothingly.

Serena grimaced and sighed. "Well, there's nothing to be done about it now. Ciardis, meet Sarah, the Head Archivist for the Guild. She registers each and every recruit, trainee, and full companion, along with their past and present domiciles, annual salary, and their magical and/or mundane talents. She'll fit you in to the roster." She gestured for Ciardis to step forward. "Your training begins tonight. There's much to learn."

From that moment on, Ciardis's day was a whirlwind of constant movement. Sarah took her in hand and quickly explained the bureaucracy and regulations of living in the Companions' Guild. "First of all, you need to know that the Companions' Guild is run by the Companions Council. The council consists of seven individuals, five female and two male, all of whom are active companions with well-established patrons."

Male companions? I didn't know about those. I wonder if they're for women, or maybe even for men, Ciardis thought with shock.

As they walked along the hallway Ciardis took in the beautiful gardens through the colonnade. Sarah continued, "The Guild keeps detailed records of each of the companions who are bound to a patron, they are known as patron companions. These patron companions are able to provide the Companions' Guild with political and financial support for council ventures in various ways. You never know who will come in handy. Who your patron is," she said as they walked across a wide, tiled hallway, "will determine who *you* are."

She took a set of keys from her belt and slipped one into the large metal lock of the left hardwood door before them. As the doors swung open, Ciardis saw a long hallway filled with door after door, presumably rooms or exits to other hallways.

"There are twenty-six rooms here," said Sarah. "Enough for each recruit on the roster. Of course, we hope all of our recruits go on to the next step in the process and become full-fledged trainees. The decision of the Companions Council will decide that though."

Ciardis nodded. "Of course."

They stopped in the middle of the hallway, at Room Five B. "This is your room," Sarah said. "The east side of the hallway is reserved for companion recruits and trainees without magic, like yourself. The A rooms, on the west, are reserved for those with magical talents."

Ciardis's eyes widened with shock, and she stuttered, "B-but Serena said that wasn't possible."

"I'm sure she said no such thing," Sarah said flatly. "She might have implied that magical companions succeed most often, and she's right. Patrons prefer companions who are useful. But that's not to say that there isn't the occasional Patron—particularly those with no gifts of their own—who prefer a companion who can maintain the books, organize the household, or even school their children."

In her thoughts Ciardis highlighted on, "*maintain the books, organize, school.*"

"That's not a companion, that's a wife," muttered Ciardis.

"What?" Sarah asked sharply as she unlocked the door.

"Nothing," said Ciardis hastily. "Just talking to myself."

 30

Ciardis walked into her new quarters behind Sarah, taking in the layout with wide eyes. This room was bigger than the kitchen at the inn in Vaneis! There was a four-poster bed, an armoire, a desk, a storage nook, and—at this point, she gasped aloud—*an attached bathroom.* Sarah followed her as she wandered around in amazement, touching objects and gazing at them with wonder.

When Ciardis looked questioningly at the five knobs of varying sizes and shapes over the tiled bathing nook, Sarah showed her which one to turn to summon the water, and explained the symbols above each knob: soap, hair lather, perfume, and cleanser.

Sarah said, "Now, this is all very nice, but you must realize that it all comes at a price. You must be accepted as a trainee, and then you must succeed in the Patron Hunt—only then can you enter contract under the Guild's name." Her eyes narrowed. "We ensure that the financial cost of housing you, feeding you, training you and clothing you is paid either way. You will either be charged a sum upon signing your contract with a patron or be required to repay the Companions' Guild upon exit from companion training."

That sounded ominous. Ciardis nodded mutely.

Sarah sat on the bed and stared at Ciardis, who stood there meekly. "So tell me, what did you study in Vaneis? The basics? Instruments? Languages?"

Ciardis shook her head, feeling ashamed. "I only know a little arithmetic, ma'am, and how to do laundry."

Sarah rubbed her eyes in irritation with a sigh. "Oh dear. Serena's been known to be taken in by a pretty face, but even she couldn't be this idiotic. There must be something…" Shifting to reach into her pocket and then turning back to Ciardis with a metal locket in her hand, Sarah asked, "Do you know why I am the Master Archivist for the Companions' Guild?"

Ciardis responded tentatively, "Because you're good at reading and writing?"

Sarah responded with a wry smile. "Yes. I also have a great memory and an empathic touch. The latter will be a trait that is most useful to us right now."

Ciardis bit her lip and nervously bunched a bit of her dress in her hand. "What's an empathic touch?" she finally asked.

Before answering, Sarah reached over to ease Ciardis's grip on her dress and smoothed over the wrinkled fabric. "My dear, that's a sign of nervousness that you need to get over," Sarah said sardonically.

"Now," she continued, "Empathy is the ability to feel memories and composition. It is usually not done through physical feelings but I can assess the memories only through touch. I am not a mind healer, but rather a visualizer."

"Right," murmured Ciardis.

Sarah nodded and said, "Usually, this means I can touch a book or scroll in the library and the essence of it will imprint on me. I'll instantly know a vague sense of the contents. It's better if I read it, of course."

Sarah continued, "The Companions Council recently discovered that I am also able to read human visualizations to see what their abilities are or might be." She glanced away briefly. "We tried it with a non-human—a *kialis,* which is practically human anyway—but, well, that didn't go so well."

After a long, expressionless moment, Sarah went on. "Regardless, I can tell what talents, if any, a person is imbued with. It's usually an art form, such as the ability to play one or more instruments, or dance. Or sometimes it's a gift for numbers and figures. That one is always a favorite with the newly rich."

Ciardis clasped her hands in front of her chest. "You might be able to read me, then!" she said excitedly. "Perhaps I have a talent!"

"Yes," said Sarah approvingly. "Now sit down, please."

 32

CHAPTER FOUR

Ciardis sat and dropped her hands into her lap, ready for anything, as long as she found out what her talent was, if any. Sarah took off her spectacles and tucked back behind her ears the wisps of hair that were fluttering in her face. Then she straightened up and put her hands on either side of Ciardis's face.

"Hmm," she said after five long minutes. Ciardis frowned. There'd been no magic spark or rustling winds or anything.

Where was the magical flash of power? Wasn't that how you could tell a mage from a mundane? Ciardis hoped the lack of magical excitement didn't mean anything. Perhaps Sarah's empathic touch wasn't meant to be a visual demonstration?

Ciardis peered anxiously at Sarah's face, hoping for a clue.

"I don't believe it," Sarah whispered finally. In a slightly louder voice, she asked, "What did you say your full name was?"

"Ciardis Rafaela Vane."

Sarah said quickly, "And it *is* your true name, registered by the hands of your mother and father?"

TERAH EDUN

Ciardis nodded anxiously. "They went to the birth archives in the town and everything. Named me after the town, in a way. At least, that's what I've been told."

"Then someone misled you. Or deliberately lied." Sarah stared at her intently and abruptly stood, "Come with me now!"

They rushed out of Ciardis's room and into the dorm hallway, Sarah clasping Ciardis's hand as they ran. They passed through three different corridors along the way. Ciardis barely saw a glimpse of the intricate artwork and beautiful statues in the halls as she rushed around corners – trying to keep up with Sarah's fast pace. Soon they came to an abrupt stop in front of a large door. At the top of the door in scrolled letters was inscribed, "*The Companions Library.*" As they entered, Sarah asked in a hoarse whisper, "Do you recall what the first part of my mage gift is?"

Ciardis nodded and said, "A photographic memory." She tried to ignore the trembling in Sarah's hands as the archivist led her through the bookcases. For her part Sarah would stop in the middle of the library aisles and turn in a circle while pulling Ciardis with her.

Occasionally Sarah's hand would tighten on Ciardis's as she cast her gaze around her like a bloodhound on the hunt. Sarah was searching with her magic for something…what exactly that was Ciardis couldn't say. Seeing the girl's confusion Sarah explained, "I'm sending out feelers from my mage core in different directions hoping to sense the manuscript that most feels like your mage core."

"My mage core?" questioned Ciardis, "I have one?"

"Oh, most definitely," said Sarah in a grim tone, "I would question how you didn't know about it before this."

After a few minutes of this, Sarah instructed Ciardis in a whisper, "The imprints that I'm sending feelers out for are like markers. If it's in a book, I can trace the marker back to its source. With my memory and the imprint trail, I never forget where I've placed a book."

After a moment of silence she continued, "Your imprint reminds me strongly of a book I read long ago, as a child. If I'm right, there hasn't been a companion trainee of your type in more than thirty years."

"Um...my 'type?'"

"Ah ha!" said Sarah triumphantly as she turned so that her body faced south. She began to rush off into the direction of the back corner of the library stacks. She stopped directly in front of a red leather-bound book with gold lettering on the front. She dropped Ciardis's hand to pull the book off of the shelf with both hands. She held it reverently. As she turned to face Ciardis, she said, "This book...it feels just like your imprint. There's no mistaking it!"

"And what does that mean?" Ciardis asked.

Sarah looked up from gazing upon the pages of the book. The pages crinkled with the stiffness of calfskin under her hands. "That means that the book is the essence of what your talent is about."

Ciardis's eyes widened as she hesitantly reached to take hold of the book. Her hands were shaking now, she noticed in wry irony. She turned the front cover towards her as Sarah said aloud, "The title is *The History of the Weathervanes.*"

"Weathervanes? You mean like the metal roosters and flying pigs on the roofs of buildings? Why is that special?"

"No, no—*Weathervane* is a sense of identity not an object," snapped Sarah. "Heavens above, didn't you learn anything in that little village of yours?"

"I...well...yes," said Ciardis in a small voice. "Just not this."

Sarah loosed an irritated sigh, "It's right there in your surname. You were *not* named after some silly little town. The Weathervanes are a family that hasn't had a known descendant in decades. They were thought extinct; the last daughter disappeared twenty years ago. Their talent was to seek and magnify the magical talents of others."

Ciardis's mouth widened, "So...I *don't* have magic myself?"

Sarah looked flabbergasted. "My dear girl, you have *more* than magic—you have the ability to *enhance* magic. That talent will be sought by many." The archivist shut her mouth and stared at Ciardis hard. At last, she said, "Tonight, your assignment is to read this book from cover to cover. I won't tolerate any stupid questions when you start your tutorials."

Ciardis gulped and nodded nervously. "Yes, ma'am."

"Come," Sarah said, "I'll take you back to your quarters."

Ciardis grew progressively paler as she followed Sarah silently through the corridors. She'd been so eager to please Sarah that she'd forgotten to tell her that she had another problem: she couldn't read.

After Sarah left, Ciardis stared down hopelessly at the book in her hands. This book held the key to her new life in its pages, and she knew that if she didn't read it tonight, she'd be kicked out of tutorials tomorrow, maybe even sent back to Vaneis in disgrace.

No one wants an idiot companion trainee, she thought ruefully. She was in over her head, and she had no idea what she could do about it.

An hour after she'd returned to her room, there was a sharp knock at her door. Ciardis jumped and went to open it. Perhaps it was Sarah. Maybe now Ciardis could tell her the embarrassing truth about why she could not complete her assignment. She could leave before the mocking jeers even started.

To both her relief and dismay, it was not Sarah at her door, but a blonde lass with blue eyes and a sour expression on her face. "Hi," said the young woman sharply, her hands on her hips and her foot tapping erratically.

"Hello," Ciardis said a little warily, "May I help you?"

The girl sighed dramatically and said, "Yes! You can quit your bellyaching. It's keeping me awake." The girl turned around with a swish of her blue nightdress and started to walk back across the hall.

Ciardis looked at her retreating back in disbelief, not sure how to respond.

A small laugh from the shadows shook her out of a stupor. Another young woman stood across the hall in front of Room Three A. Ciardis's mouth pressed into a thin line; she felt anger toward both the girl who'd just insulted her and the girl laughing at her from the shadows of her doorway. This new girl was wearing tight black men's clothing, and was clearly mocking Ciardis.

Ciardis decided to call out to the first one, "I don't know what your problem is, but I haven't disturbed anybody. In fact, I haven't said a word in over an hour."

The girl whirled and sneered. "You stupid peasant! I'm a *telepath,* which means I can hear any thoughts you project!"

"Well, goody for you, then! Listen to this!" Ciardis yelled, slamming her door. She slumped against the doorframe. She had honestly had no idea what else to say. *Besides,* she thought, *let the girl suffer for one night.* Ciardis would probably be kicked out by morning, anyway. *Stupid, rich, magical, stuck-up, snotty girl,* she ranted in her head. She hoped the telepath had heard that, too.

Ciardis got to her feet as another knock came from the other side of her door. She rolled her eyes, opened it, and snarled, "What now, you insipid…"

She trailed off when she saw the other girl in front of her—the one who had been laughing at her from the shadows. Changing her statement mid-sentence she began again, "What do you want?"

"You know, you *could* be nicer," said the girl, while leaning against the doorframe.

"And why should I?" Ciardis asked sharply.

"Because I might be able to help you with your problem. Your assignment was something to do with reading a book, right?"

Ciardis blinked. "How would you know that?"

"Patricia was ranting for a full ten minutes in the hallway about your 'inconsiderate nature' before she knocked on your door," the girl said.

"Well," said Ciardis, suddenly flustered, "I...um... Come in." She motioned the other girl forward and shut the door.

"I'm Stephanie," said the girl. Ciardis nodded and offered her name.

"What did you mean about helping me?" she asked quickly.

"First, what is your problem exactly?" replied Stephanie. "I need to hear it from you." She had moved to stand next to the armoire. Ciardis stood near the bed. The two of them together couldn't have been more different. Stephanie wasn't dressed like a proper woman in a skirt or a dress. She was dressed in tight black leather pants that defined her legs and a light black cotton shirt that stretched over her chest. She wore a simple copper pendant around her neck, and her slick black hair was pulled up into an elegant chignon at the back of her head. Ciardis noted her style with incredulity – not quite sure what to think of it but knowing that back in the vale she would be stoned for the impropriety.

Ciardis bit her lip and sighed as she picked up the red book. "I can't read," she admitted, "and I need the ability in order to learn about my heritage."

The other girl rolled her eyes. "Is that *all*?" she asked in the snootiest tone imaginable.

Ciardis snarled. She might have to take insults from Sarah, but *not* from these girls. "Not all of us grew up with silver spoons in our mouths," she retorted.

"Right," responded Stephanie. "Look, don't get your knickers in a bunch. What I meant was that my magical talent is transfers— sometimes called 'copying.'"

 38

"Copying?" asked Ciardis, sitting down slowly. She was beginning to feel a headache coming on.

The girl raised an eyebrow. "I can transfer skills to another person for a limited time. The talent I copy is usually a skill that I transfer from one person to another. It also can be a personal skill that I've learned over time – the *hard* way. How long a skill transfer lasts depends on the complexity of the skill. For instance, combat skill transfers only last a few weeks. Something as basic as reading—in *one* language, mind you—will last you for years. Enough time for you to pick it up on your own."

"Oh my," said Ciardis shakily, "That's quite the talent."

"I know," said the girl smugly.

"Well, yes, then," said Ciardis. "If you're offering, I'd be glad to have your help."

"Nothing is free," Stephanie replied. "What can you give me in return?"

Ciardis stared at Stephanie in amazement, thinking that the manners of the people in this city were atrocious.

"Well?" repeated Stephanie. "I don't have all night."

Ciardis quickly gathered her thoughts. "What do you want? I have some dresses," she said, reaching for the packages that Serena had acquired in Lineaus.

"Frilly dresses aren't really my thing."

"Well, I have nothing else to offer," snapped Ciardis. "A few coins. Laundry services."

"Laundry services?" said Stephanie with definite interest.

Ciardis's eyes narrowed as she looked at the girl. If Stephanie had been a fox, her ears would have cocked forward in curiosity at Ciardis's mention of the two words. "Yes, I was a laundress back home," Ciardis replied, grimacing inwardly at the title.

"*Now* you're talking," said Stephanie. "How about one year of reading skills transfer in exchange for a year of laundry service?"

"Six months."

"Six months of what?" asked Stephanie.

"I can learn all I need to know from you in six months," replied Ciardis with a lift of her chin and a glint in her eye. "Six months of reading skills in the Common Tongue for six months of laundry service."

Stephanie shrugged and held out her hand for a shake. Ciardis spit in her palm and swiftly slapped Stephanie's hand with her own to seal the bargain. She gasped when their hands touched. There was a sharp tingle, almost like a jolt running up her arm.

Stephanie dropped her hand and said, "Now you can read."

Stephanie walked to the door and opened it, turning around before leaving. "I would stop spitting in people's hands before you get to the Patron Hunt, if I were you," she advised. The door shut softly behind her.

Ciardis sighed and dropped back on the bed. "So many rules," she muttered to herself. She picked up the book and noted that her reading skills had already kicked in: the title was legible now, no longer just so many angular golden sticks. A small smile bloomed on her face. She'd wanted to be able to read since she was a small child and had seen the traveling bands selling books to the wealthy folk in town.

Carefully, she cracked open the red book. On the first page was an inscription:

- The History of the Family of the Weathervanes -
A Noble Clan with Powers Above All

She began to read the crisp, blocky text, noting immediately that the history of the clan—*her* clan!—extended all the way back to

Emperor Favian IV, often written Favian Stormlord, over three hundred years ago. Indeed, it was Favian who had bestowed the name Weathervane upon the clan of companions who had the extraordinary ability to amplify the magical talents of others.

As she turned the page, a wrinkled piece of manuscript floated out. Frowning, Ciardis picked it up from the bedspread where it had landed beside her.

> *I stumbled upon a young girl this morning. One of fair skin and bright laugh. She was running in the rain – a light sprinkle really. I was alone, leaving my retinue on the ridge. As she came forward she stumbled falling to my feet. By accident her sandy hand touched my bare feet. And a miracle was born.*
>
> *– Recitation from His Imperial Highness, Prince Favian*

The account went on in detail. It told of a brilliant summer storm and Prince Favian's powerful surge of magic after a touch of the girl's hands. Under the rain, he had increased the strength of the storm from a sprinkle of rain to a storm of incredible power. After that, he had used the girl to stoke his power like a metal weathervane draws lightning in a storm.

He used the nickname of "Weathervane" for the girl, and it became a common way to refer to her, and later, her children who possessed the same skill.

Female weathervanes became known for their abilities to enhance not only the powers of their chosen partners, but their focused output. But the male weathervanes were more erratic – it was hard to tell if they would connect to a partner or be able to enhance at all. Some male weathervanes became powerful enough to enhance the magical output of entire groups of people but only when all the individuals were present which was less useful.

She frowned as she read about her ancestors exploits in *The History of the Family of the Weathervanes*. They'd been generals, companions, princes, lesser nobles, and—at this she raised an eyebrow—thieves. *That's interesting*, she thought as she read up more on Kieran, the Weathervane thief-lord who had put together a synchronized crew of thieves whose exploits had been legendary.

In the middle of the book was a family timeline. Beside each name was a brief physical description: silver hair, blonde hair, black hair; olive skin, pale skin, cinnamon skin, and dark skin. But every one person described had at least one feature in common - golden eyes.

Just like mine.

The last Weathervane to have been born was a girl, Lily, thirty-seven years before. She'd had black hair and cinnamon-colored skin, according to the text. *My mother had black hair, too*, Ciardis thought with excitement. It was one of the few things she could remember about her.

As she carefully read the rest of the entry, she read a small paragraph that stated that female mages were always named after their mothers. In fact, girl children always took the second half of their parents' names.

> *For example Erin Stonebreaker, was known as Erin Breaker before her fifteenth birthday. Upon gaining her powers she received the full titular right to claim the whole last name. It is the same for Weathervanes. Each child, male or female, is given the name of Vane on their birth records. They are only allowed to change this name upon manifestation of their powers.*

Sitting up Ciardis realized that her mother had done the same for her. She had named her *Ciardis Vane* after her family not after Vaneis. Males—even Mages—took the latter half of their female partner's name.

> *A continued example of male child names would be Marx Breaker. He took the last name of his wife Erin Stonebreaker, as all men do – magical or mundane. Prior to their marriage, he was known as Marx Chemist, Chemist being the name of his mother.*

After two hours of reading, she closed the book with a tired sigh. Looking out the window, she noted that the dawn would come in just four short hours. She needed sleep. After changing into a nightdress and putting the book carefully on the desk, she curled up in the center of the big bed. With a wry smile, she sank into the mattress, thinking, *I could get used to this.*

CHAPTER FIVE

She woke to find a stranger bustling about her room. "Rise and shine!" the woman said cheerfully as she dusted the armoire.

Ciardis sat up in alarm, rubbing her eyes carefully. She frowned at the woman, who was wearing what was clearly a maid's uniform and wielding a stick with a bunch of feathers tied to one end. "What are you doing?" she asked curiously.

The woman cast her an amused glance and said, "Why, I'm dusting, obviously." Ciardis decided not to question it further, and swung her feet over the edge of the bed. "There's breakfast for you in the common gardens," the woman said.

"Thank you," said Ciardis. "How do I get there?"

"Go out the door, turn right, walk down the hall, turn left, go down the spiral staircase, and you'll be right in the gardens. Can't miss it!"

Ciardis dressed and followed her directions, as well as the aroma that led her straight to a laden breakfast table. As she wandered over to it, she admired the beauty surrounding her. The garden was laid

44

out in a quadrant pattern, with low-cut grass and small rocks as boundaries. A high hedge surrounded the whole garden except for a long opening opposite the staircase.

Grabbing some fresh fruit and fried bread, she stepped toward the opening in the garden hedge. It looked down onto the beach she'd noticed yesterday, and she gasped aloud as she took in the striking sight of the turquoise waves lapping at the sand. After a while, she returned to the table, picking the chair nearest to the ocean.

Soon, a girl with thick braids looped across her head and down her back joined her at the table. "Beautiful, isn't it?" she asked.

"Yes," replied Ciardis softly, "It is."

"No matter how long I'm here, I know I'll never tire of this view," the girl said. "I'm Terris, sponsored by Vana," she said, offering her hand.

Ciardis turned to her, surprised, and shook her hand. She recognized the sponsor – the one Serena had called a harridan. "Ciardis, sponsored by Serena. Are you from the Summer Isles?"

"Yes," said Terris, smiling a shy smile. "You know that my sponsor hates yours, right?"

"I got that impression," Ciardis said tentatively while munching on a piece of bread. They looked at each other and burst into giggles. They started chatting and barely noticed when others joined them. Their conversation stretched on until the sound of a bell rang throughout the garden.

A woman stood at the head of the table, clearly waiting for their attention. After a few minutes of waiting she announced, "Welcome, young recruits, to the Companions' Guild. Your tutorials will begin in five minutes. You can meet your sponsor in the main hall."

The recruits eagerly got up to go to the main hall. As soon as Ciardis saw Serena, the first thing out of her mouth was, "What's the difference between a wife and a consort?"

45

Ciardis clasped her hand over her mouth. She'd been wondering all night, but she hadn't meant to blurt it out like that. Fortunately, Serena seemed amused. "Good question! You're jumping right in, I see. Walk with me."

They exited the grand hall to a small path that led down to the beach. Along the way, Serena explained, "A consort is a contractual partner - they hold power and rank equal to their spouse's. If you are Queen Consort, you are so much more than just a Queen. A spouse, on the other hand, is a husband or wife. They hold only the power personally delegated to them by their partner. A Consort maintains all of the power that their partner does with no restrictions."

"Oh," said Ciardis, "That sounds quite complicated."

"It is," Serena replied. "But in situations where a companion is being considered for the rank of consort or even spouse, the Companions' Guild will advise on the structure of the partnership and contractual agreement to serve." She waved a dainty hand. "But enough of those matters for now. That is far ahead in your future." She clapped her hands excitedly. "Sarah tells me you're one of the long-lost Weathervanes! I just knew it!"

Is that why you called me "baseborn" on our way here, then?

"My dear this changes everything!" said Serena, ignoring Ciardis's silence as she twirled around.

"How so?" inquired Ciardis. "I mean, I know about the—my—family history, but it usually takes a while for a girl's gifts to manifest, right? None of my female ancestors were able to enhance before their eighteenth birthdays."

Serena stopped twirling. "You *have* been studying. That's very good!" she said, turning to face Ciardis, her finger at her lips.

Ciardis resented being spoken to like a toddler, but once again held her tongue.

"Look, this is how it goes," Serena said in a no-nonsense tone.

"Now that we know you *have* a talent—and it's an exceedingly rare one at that—either you will automatically be accepted as a companion trainee, and we'll accelerate your tutorials to prepare you for your Coming Out ceremony at the Patron Hunt, or we'll gently start informing eligible patrons of your unique gifts."

At this, Serena clasped her hands together, "The turnout will be *spectacular*. Everyone will want to see the new Weathervane – especially the mages."

Ciardis gave a weak grin. She was excited, she really was, but she couldn't help but remember all those ancestors mentioned in the book whose gifts hadn't ever manifested. What would happen if hers didn't?

"Now," said Serena, ticking off points on her fingers, "Before the Patron Hunt, you'll need to take Dance, Defense, Manners, and Practicals. I'll hire a transfer mage to copy the Sahalian language in you, as well. These tutorials will be crucial to your success at the Patron Hunt. You must impress viable candidates with your composure. What are your personal attributes?" asked Serena, beaming.

"I have no idea what you mean by that," Ciardis said without hesitation.

Frowning Serena rephrased while moving her hand in an encouraging manner, "What are the things that you're *good* at?"

"Reading," said Ciardis quickly.

Serena flicked off the example. "Oh, so boring! The correct answer is 'hunting, darts, and riding.'"

Ciardis stared at her in wide-eyed horror.

Laughing, Serena said, "Really, dear, we must buy you a sense of humor. Just a little joke. But seriously, we'll have to come up with a better list than just 'reading.'"

Serena stopped, looking over Ciardis's shoulder. Ciardis looked around, raising her hand to shade her eyes from the sun's glare. The bright rays shining down made the castle sparkle with waves of pink, but she wasn't fooled. The glare felt ominous, like the stone walls held secrets that were creeping up on her, step by step, while blinding her with its beauty.

A small, slender man was gliding toward them across the sand. He wore silky gray pants and a tan vest over a long-sleeved white shirt. Serena was clearly appreciating his physique, and Ciardis couldn't help but think, *He must be so warm in that outfit.*

As he approached, Serena said, "Ciardis, may I present your tutorials instructor for the Patron Hunt, Damias Lancer." At his shallow bow, she continued, "Damias is the finest tutorial instructor in the Guild. If anyone can get you prepared for the Patron Hunt in three months' time, he can."

A small smile eased onto Damias's face. "Lady Serena exaggerates, but I will do my best to make you the greatest candidate presented at the Patron Hunt this season." He clapped his hands together. "Now, shall we get off this dreadful sand? We'll begin with your Dance tutorial inside."

They headed off the beach and into an empty ballroom, where Ciardis proceeded to learn the first ballroom dance steps for what felt like hours. It was surprisingly exhausting, and the dances were completely unlike the sprightly village dances she already knew. When they finished, after several encouraging remarks from Damias—although she swore she heard Serena mutter from the sidelines something about storks who couldn't dance—they transitioned to Defense.

Defense was probably better described as "how to hide pointy things in your dress and curtsy without stabbing yourself," but it was actually quite fun. They went over how to conceal knives in various garments, keeping sharpened needles tipped with sleeping potions in her hair, and Ciardis's favorite: a fan with spikes that extended outward with a push of a button. Damias cautioned her that the fan was an absolute last resort in battle, and would be given to her only after she'd mastered the *katas*, the formal military dances associated with its use.

"The Manners tutorial will be held over lunch," Damias said when they were done. "Serena and I will instruct you in the etiquette of noble meals, while feasting on the finest dishes offered in the Guild."

Damias picked up two clear goblets and set them before her. Then he laid out five eating utensils along with two napkins.

"The napkins I understand, but why do I need two goblets and five pieces of silverware?"

He picked up both goblets, holding one in each hand. "The slender goblet will always be for wine. The larger goblet will take water for you to drink with your meal. If you wish to signal a server that you desire no further refills, simply place the smaller napkin upon the glass."

Serena said, "And, of course, each of these utensils serves a purpose." She picked them up one by one as she explained. "These are the salad fork, the meat fork, the dessert fork, the carving knife, and the butter knife. If you happen to need a spoon, it will be served with the appropriate course."

"In Vaneis, we only had one utensil besides a knife," said Ciardis, carefully memorizing the name and placement of each utensil. "It was round-bottomed with three tines."

"We have those here, too," Damias said with a smile. "Though you'll rarely see them in a noble's house, and then only in the lower kitchens. They're called foons."

"What a ridiculous sounding name," tutted Serena.

"Another thing," said Damias, carefully wiping his mouth with his napkin. "Always be aware of what you're drinking. Only accept drinks from prospective Patrons or the servers."

"In the past a few trainee companions have gone to great lengths to ensure a successful match," interjected Serena. "Actions which we find deplorable were taken – including use of poisons to get rid of potential rivals."

"In addition to conventional methods like poisoning, several trainees – who have since been removed from the Companions' Guild – *spelled* a hallway in the guild by pouring their magic into the walls and causing another trainee walking the halls to have hallucinations. The perceptions were so vivid visually and mentally that she believed she was drowning. She believed it so much that she stopped breathing because her lungs couldn't retain enough air even though the hallway was perfectly normal."

Damias pursed his mouth in distaste. "I hope I never hear of such a thing happening with you, Ciardis."

"No, of course not!"

After lunch, Serena escorted Ciardis to the barter station in town. Serena took her up to an older man with rheumy eyes. He wore nondescript clothing and leaned on a cane. Serena said to Ciardis, "This is the only registered copier in ten miles. He's also deaf."

Serena leaned over and picked up a small piece of parchment with scribbles on it. She neatly wrote out, *The Sahalian language.*

Once they have finished negotiating a suitable rate, she paid him one hundred and fifty shillings for two years of knowledge. He touched Ciardis's shoulder, and she felt the same electric jolt that Stephanie had given her the night before and suddenly she was thinking in the difficult Dragonkin tongue.

As they walked away, Serena muttered to Ciardis, "He's blind, practically deaf, and getting senile. I'll be so glad when that recruit, Stephanie, finally masters her copying talent. It cannot come a day too soon."

Ciardis asked casually, "Masters? Is she not already talented?"

"Oh, she is," assured Serena, "But she needs the seal of approval from the Talents Guild before she can practice and sell her skills at the Barter station or to private consumers. Though, she only has two more weeks before her Talents exam, since she was selected by a superb Patron this past fall."

Ciardis decided not to mention Stephanie's unapproved talent transfer from the night before.

"Once you've been selected by a patron as their companion, you'll go before the Talents Guild, as well," Serena said.

From then on, time passed quickly with Ciardis's Dance and Defense tutorials, measurements for ball gowns, dinner staging, and tutoring in art appreciation, household arrangements and decorative arts.

***

As her sixth week of tutorials came to a close, Ciardis ruefully remembered her hope for a new life, away from bullies and hard labor.

Today had been proof that everything and nothing had changed.

She'd managed to run into Patricia again, and this time, the girl's telepathic snit wasn't a small affair.

Ciardis had been minding her own business in one of the outer gardens, practicing the different levels of curtsies given to a person depending on their social status. Her knees were bent and her skirt was spread on the ground, when a stiff breeze unbalanced her. She tumbled to the ground and her skirts flew over her head.

As she quickly righted herself and brushed her hair from her face she heard laughter erupt from behind her. In the shadows of the garden entrance, two girls and a young man stood clearly mocking her. The girl next to Patricia was mimicking her fall with an exaggerated face and arms milling widely about for balance.

The boy next to her was silently watching as a wind came down from the sky and began to twist around him so that he stood inside his own whirlwind. He watched her with calculating eyes and Ciardis knew that he had been the cause of her fall. The winds around them now and before were nowhere near strong enough to push over a person without a mage's help.

Ciardis's faced flamed with embarrassment, but she couldn't run. They were standing in the middle of the only path back to safety and her room.

With nowhere to go and no way to avoid them, she raised her head high, her chin trembling, and grabbed a bunch of her dress in both hands to keep her hands from shaking with tremors.

"You know," said Patricia with a hint of cruelty in her voice, "If you really wanted to learn how to pay respect to the ground, I would have had Terris show you."

Going stiff with ire at the girl's dig at her friend, Ciardis retorted, "It takes a dirt kisser to know one, Patricia. Perhaps *you* should teach me."

The young man at Patricia's side quickly stifled a laugh with a cough into his fist.

Patricia's charming smile transformed into a frown to rival the anger of the legendary Bella Mickens—a girl Ciardis knew from back home in Vaneis who *nobody* messed with. Ciardis cringed and ducked instinctively, ready for the blow to hit her, completely forgetting her defense training.

But she had underestimated Patricia. She wouldn't hit anyone; the risk of marring her manicure was too great.

"At least I'm not some gold digging baseborn bitch," the girl said viciously. "Go back to where you came from—you won't find a husband there, either, but it's better than the humiliation you'll receive here."

She turned around, stepped around her companions, and swept off in a huff without a backwards glance, leaving Ciardis with tears running down her face.

Patricia's friends followed right behind her leaving Ciardis to wonder how this person far removed from her life up North had found out about her broken relationship with Fervis Miller.

Was nothing a secret here? *Nothing of mine is*, she thought ruefully.

After some dramatic dirt kicking, which left the garden looking like a lawn gnome had decided to redecorate, Ciardis went back to her room.

"And to think I thought they'd be nice here," she muttered to herself, then sighed and collapsed on her fluffy bed. Spreading her hands over the mattress, she couldn't help but smile as she remembered her room back in Vaneis. Living in this castle was worlds above the small freezing inn where even with a heat spell the nights were cold and the blankets too thin. Flipping over and putting her hands behind her head she reminisced over the lessons from the past two months. It seemed never-ending - there was always something she didn't know.

Damias was a difficult taskmaster, but she could tell he was making every effort to prepare her for her Hunt, although sometimes she wondered if he planned for her to die of exhaustion before she even got there.

Hearing a knock at her door, she rolled over onto her back and shouted, "Come in." Sitting up, she couldn't help but hope it wasn't Patricia; she didn't need more trouble today.

It wasn't Patricia, thank goodness. Terris stood in the doorway, bearing cakes.

"Phew," said Ciardis, "I'm just glad you're not Patricia…or Stephanie, for that matter."

She hadn't seen Stephanie in weeks. After Stephanie had passed the Talents Guild test four weeks ago, she'd moved into an apartment of her own in the city. No doubt she was insanely busy preparing to take over from the ancient Master Copier at the Barter Hall.

But she had been *so* thoughtful and arranged to have a local woman continue to deliver her dirty laundry to Ciardis's doorstep once a week like clockwork.

Ciardis gave Terris a grin and patted the bed. They'd become fast friends over the past few weeks.

"Stephanie, I get. She's got an intense laundry situation, that one. I swear the last pile that woman brought over was taller AND wider than me," said Terris. "But Patricia?"

Ciardis quickly filled her in on that morning's events.

Terris set the box of soft cakes on the bed between them and they proceeded to divvy up the spoils. Ciardis went for the delectable caramel rolls—soft cake drizzled with sweet honey and caramel sauce—because they reminded her of winter back home. Terris preferred the brown ginger cakes for their hint of sweetness and overall snap.

"I saw you dancing with Lord Damias in the solar today," Terris said.

Ciardis groaned aloud before Terris could utter another word. "No, I didn't mean it that way. You're not so bad. I mean…you're getting better!" Terris said. "Sailor's honor."

"You mean I only stepped on his toes three times and tripped him once, right?"

"Yeah," admitted Terris with a wry grin, "That about covers it."

Ciardis rolled her eyes and popped another morsel into her mouth. Through the mouthful of cake, she said, "I don't know how they expect me to memorize all those dances by the Patron Hunt! I'm going to look like a bumbling fool, I just know it!" Sulkily, she muttered, "Why can't they just hire a copier to instill it in me?"

"You know why," said Terris sternly. "A skill like dancing costs ten thousand shillings, because they can't just give you one dance—it must be all of them. Besides, there are only two copiers in all of Sandrin presently, and neither of them can dance worth anything."

"What? How did Stephanie pass her Patron Hunt if she couldn't dance?"

"Well, technically she can dance to music—it's just not up to the skill of her sword dancing," Terris explained. "The Companions' Guild decided in her pre-Hunt interview that she should stick to the swords, since her prospective Patrons all professed an interest in the subject."

"Right," Ciardis murmured.

"You, on the other hand," said Terris as she playfully lobbed some popped corn kernels in Ciardis's direction, "don't have a primary *or* a secondary talent to rely on and must learn what you can before the Hunt starts."

"That's not true!" argued Ciardis. "I can make a mean snow cone!"

"Snow cone? What's a snow cone?"

After Ciardis explained the treat, Terris burst out laughing and didn't stop for a full five minutes. Ciardis sat glaring at her, her legs crossed as she leaned back against a bunch of pillows. "It's a serious talent," she said stiffly.

"Uh huh," said Terris, still chuckling. "Do you see any snow around here?"

Ciardis rolled her eyes. "Maybe one of my prospective Patrons will be a Winter Lord or a Weather Mage. I *am* a Weathervane, after all."

"You know your abilities to enhance will extend beyond the capacity to increase weather-related magic," Terris pointed out.

"I know," said Ciardis, "But my ancestors book makes the ability to enhance weather sound pretty awesome."

Terris sighed and said, "I also hoped to have a patron who hailed from my homeland in the Summer Isles, but most of the Patrons come from these or nearby lands. Now, time to get down to business. Who's that cute guy down the hall?"

At this, Ciardis burst out laughing herself. "Terris? You have a crush on him, don't you? I knew it!"

"Maybe," said Terris with a little giggle as she twisted some of her braids around a finger. "He's so cute! I can't help it. Blond hair, blue eyes, tight physique."

Ciardis shook her head. "What a pair you two would make, with your dark skin and his fair skin."

Terris grinned. "You know it!"

CHAPTER SIX

Later that night, Ciardis sat alone at her desk, studying. She had to catch up on all the practical material Damias had given her.

The focus of the Practicals shifted between the magical and the mundane every week, which made her happy—she never knew what was next. They had flown through mind-focusing for memory retention, mind-shielding—*Note to self: get better at it, Patricia kicked your ass today*, she thought—and Sahalian texts. This week was mathematics, which she found quite interesting.

Damias had also stressed the importance of being able to take over the operation of her Patron's manor from the start. At the moment, she had to go over a keep's ledger – the book in which all financial transactions were kept. It included everything from overall maintenance of the building: mason work, caulking, and wood floor replacements, to purchase of grain for winter use and payment to household staff members. Next she had to review a merchant's cost estimate for new upholstery for all of the furniture throughout the entire manor, rework each of the merchant's estimates, calculate the totals and compare them to the head butler's own calculations for errors. All she could say was that these nobles must have some truly dodgy financiers. The errors were astronomical and from the inflated figures Ciardis saw once she'd compared the merchant's cost estimates and the head butler's figures – it was clear that the head butler was skimming a profit off of the top.

The comparisons took her close to two hours to complete, and then she lit a lamp to practice some simple *katas* for her defense tutorials. She worked hard day and night, not just to impress Damias and Serena, but also to ensure that she would be selected by a patron.

The prospect of the selection haunted her dreams and waking thoughts alike. She had yet to manifest her Weathervane powers, and no matter how many times she reread the book section that told her the powers would arrive only after her eighteenth birthday—if they ever did—she was still impatient. The what-ifs and doubts clouded her mind, making her belly tense with worry even in slumber. What made it worse was that her eighteenth birthday was just two weeks before the Patron Hunt was set to begin.

She had two weeks to master her powers—*if* they came in at all. Not very reassuring.

She soon noticed that she was throwing off her *katas* in her worry, and decided to go to bed. Nothing more could be accomplished tonight.

By the end of the week in her Dance class, even Damias could tell something was wrong. She could see that, but it was equally clear that he had wanted to wait and see if she could overcome whatever was troubling her before asking about it.

They were dancing a complicated quartet pattern. Serena had been kind enough to provide a set of ghostly partners for each of them.

As Ciardis wavered for the fifth time under her airy partner's guidance, Damias, ever the gentleman, signaled that he wanted to change partners. When Damias and Ciardis came together for their dance, the two ghostly partners Serena had provided dissipated as if they'd never been there. The dance of four became a dance of two with Damias leading, holding Ciardis's left hand high and wrapping an arm around her waist. They eased into a simple two-step and whirled about the ballroom to the tune of a small magical music ball playing violas in the corner. Serena, her job done and her airy visions dissipated, had pulled out a pamphlet and begun to read.

Ciardis was pretty sure that the previous dance had been invented just to show off the richness of the dancers' clothing. She was glad it was over. This one was a bit more sedate; at certain parts of the dance when Ciardis was required to look away from her partner, she was able to get a look at Serena's literature. It appeared to be a lady's pamphlet on facial powder. *I'll have to ask Serena if I can borrow it,* she thought excitedly. Then it struck her like a blow that only a few months before, such a thing would never have occurred to her, to desire makeup, to wear gowns and jewels. Those had been fantastic figments of every laundress's imagination.

But alongside the painful desire to continue in this lifestyle of luxury was the near certain feeling she had that she'd fail to manifest her powers. That, in turn, brought the issue of her powers—or lack thereof—back to the forefront of her mind, and from there it was just a downhill emotional spiral.

As the dance ended, Damias said with a chuckle, "You've done well. But you need to learn to focus on what your partner is saying with his or her body. Then you'll know which way to turn *your* body."

"I know," said Ciardis. "It's just difficult to read my partner's cues when they're nothing but ghostly shapes."

Damias grinned. "If you can learn to master the dances with a visual partner with no physical presence, then you'll be able to read the cues of a real partner with no problem."

Ciardis nodded and prepared for the next set of dance instructions. As Damias demonstrated with moving hands and flowing movements, Ciardis tried to fake a smile, but when he turned to her, a silent tear betrayed her feelings.

Damias frowned and brought his hands down. "Clearly this is about more than a dance. Sit. Let's talk." He folded himself gracefully into a crossed-legged position on the ballroom floor. Ciardis followed, tucking her legs under her in the proper ladylike equivalent of his position.

"It's my powers…" Ciardis said, her eyes closed in shame. "They haven't manifested yet. If they don't, all the Patrons will rescind their invitations."

"Ciardis," said Damias softly, "You know as well as I do that female Weathervanes have to wait longer for their powers; they invariably mature *after* their eighteenth birthdays. And it can take even longer. My partner's powers didn't even come in until her twenty-first birthday, and she's a Fire Master!"

"Yes," said Ciardis, sniffling, "But your partner is Linda Firelancer! She's…she's Imperial!"

"And does that make her different?" Damias asked.

Ciardis issued a trembling smile as he handed her his handkerchief. "I guess not." With a gulp, she looked at him. "What if I really am mundane, though? Or what if Sarah was wrong, or—"

Damias cut off her tirade with an upraised eyebrow. "Do you honestly think I would waste my time on anyone without potential? There is no way, my dear, that you are anything less than worthy of a full-fledged Patron Hunt. Besides," he said with a cocky grin, "Sarah is *never* wrong, and if she ever heard you say that she might be, she'd tear you a new hide."

60

Ciardis laughed.

"Now, I want you to take the rest of the day off. No tutorials, no family history. Just be you!" he said rising gracefully and extending a hand to help her up.

She nodded, taking his hand and pulling herself to her feet.

As she was about to turn away, he said, "Also, your patron interview is scheduled for tomorrow. All you need to do to prepare is be relaxed. The panel will be there to help you, guide you, and answer any questions you might have."

Relax, he tells me, Ciardis thought with an inward sigh as she headed back to the dorms. *Easy for him to say.*

She reached her room, a pensive expression on her face as she unlocked the door. She hesitated in the middle of the huge space, thinking about what she should do next. There was no way for her to study for the patron interview tomorrow because no assignments had been given for it and no one would tell her what it involved. She bit her lip. She'd been meaning to get a second primer from the market in the Bookbinders' District, but this week had been so busy that she'd had no time. She was already done with the first reader's primer, though, and was ready to move on to the second. Mind made up to enjoy the day and pick up another primer, she grabbed a scarf to wrap around her hair in the fashion of the season and a few coins for some small purchases.

With glee, she caught a *tuk-tuk*—a small three-wheeled conveyance that she delighted in—at the gates of the Companions' Guild and headed off into the city. It was an unseasonably warm winter, even by Sandrin standards. Usually, heavy rains came in off the sea around this time of year, but that was not so today. The heat was almost sweltering.

Deciding on her first order of business, she spotted an ice seller on her way to the bookbinders' district. She hopped out of the *tuk-*

tuk and walked. She knew that if she'd stayed with the *tuk-tuk*, the driver would drive in a large circle around to the bookbinders' district and charge her twice as much when she could just cut through the ice sellers' street.

The ice sellers' street, in the shade of large buildings, offered a shortcut through the weavers' district and into the bookbinders' district. It would also be a much cooler walk than any other route. She took out a small coin to pay the guards of the ice sellers' street, and walked between their glistening chests to be hit by a refreshing wave of cool air on the other side. The ice sellers kept their one street, which was fairly large, cool year-round by means of the services of a permanent weather mage. Contracts like this, for small streets or buildings, was lucrative work for weather mages who had to contract out their services, she imagined.

Weather mages who did contract work, known as wardens, were well received anywhere they went, but in the city of Sandrin, the Imperial Court mandated that only the two weather mages sanctioned by the Emperor could affect the weather currents and temperatures in the city. If anyone else was caught casting a major weather spell without the express written permission of the palace, it was considered a crime against the Empire and they would be punished before the courts. The only other way for a weather warden to practice in the city—aside from a few limited permits owned by certain Districts or Guilds—was to teach, which left a dearth of plump positions for those weather-inclined mages to practice in.

Which is why so many leave the city and practice on estates, Ciardis thought. Peering down at the selection of flavors she saw her favorite – strawberry! She indicated to a flavored-ice seller that she wanted it over ice chips. This delicacy was her new favorite thing about the city. She thought wistfully of the snow cones she'd told Terris about. Perhaps if she could find a way to get them to grind the ice very finely…

Aside from the flavored ice seller, the thoroughfare was packed with household ice sellers and contract sellers. Since weather wardens couldn't individually practice by cooling homes, they licensed their services to contract sellers who sold the services out by bid and paid the wardens flat fees. The contract sellers were calling out to passersby's about their services.

Two rooms – one price! said one man.

Fifteen shillings a month to keep your whole apartment cool! shouted another with a full beard.

A third voice came from behind her, *Own an inn? We give you special price! Quality cold air – day and night for your patrons.*

Soon she began tuning out the contract sellers as she continued to walk down the ice sellers' street. They were sure to make a killing piping cool air into city homes, particularly in this heat.

She had no idea how the weather wardens cooled the air in this blazing hot sun but they did it and she was eternally grateful for the Guild's contract with the contract seller who made it possible. The nights here were torrid, even with the sea breeze off the ocean. It was almost as if a heat wave was cocooned above the city.

Making her way into the Bookbinders' District took a few minutes. She finished her flavored-ice along the way, licking it carefully to avoid getting drops on her dress. She made her way between the bookshops, heading for the one that looked the most decrepit. It was a three-story building that leaned slightly to the side, like an old man with a cane, and curtains fluttered out of the windows on each floor.

As she entered the building, a small bell chimed. It was nowhere near the door – in fact it floated five feet in the air in the center of the room spelled by magic. She looked around with a smile. It looked as if more dust had collected in the four weeks since she'd last come here.

She saw that the books weren't as precariously piled as before. This time the stacks across multiple tables were no more than three or four books tall. Books took up space on floors and in the corners. The room was dark, dusty, and moldy—and she loved it. She weaved between the tables, heading for the back corner, where a small children's area was set up. The next primer was already there, bound in green cloth that designated it as Primer Two. Primer one, which she'd brought with her to trade, was bound in brown.

Gathering her new primer, she headed up to the second floor, where two of the journeyman bookbinders and the shop owner were hunched over loose pages in the filtered light. They all held thick needles in their hands as they hand-sewed the pages together. The books—or the fancy ones, anyway—wouldn't stay like that. She'd asked the owner about that on her last visit, confused as to why her primer had a proper spine and hard casing. It wasn't just sewn together with just a bit of thread. Joselin, the store owner, stood over a large desk to her right. He had told her that a formatter was brought in once a month for the fancy books. The rest were sold as-is to the outlying towns and the middle class, because you see only the richest of the city inhabitants could afford to buy even the plainest of Joselin's bound books.

She brought the second primer to Joselin with a cheerful, "Hello!"

"Hello, yourself, young lady," he said as he shifted his spectacles from the top of his head to his nose. "Ah, I see you've finished the first primer. Already?" he asked curiously, a sparkle in his eye.

She nodded eagerly, dislodging her scarf from the top of her head in the process. As she shoved it back into place, he said, "Well, I've always enjoyed seeing a young person who reads. As promised, you can trade the first primer for the second at no cost, if..." He let the end of his sentence linger.

With a small smile, Ciardis said, "If I promise to come back and teach your daughter a few dance steps."

He gave her a big smile. "Yes, this weekend will be good."

Suddenly a young girl in a tan dress came rushing down the stairs. She rushed up to Ciardis with her blonde curls flying behind her. She screeched to a stop almost on Ciardis's toes, wobbling a bit before regaining her balance. Ciardis laughed at the five-year-old girl and said, "Hello, Mala."

"Hello, Ciardis," Mala said a bit shyly as she attempted a curtsy.

"Are you ready for your lessons this weekend?" Ciardis asked with a smile.

"Yes! Papa says we can dance in the wordies' room on the third floor!" Mala said eagerly.

Ciardis hid a grin, thinking how cute Mala was. "Wordie" was Mala's word for the wordsmiths who worked in her father's shop. They created the stories and ideas that became the books he bound and sold. "Isn't that right, Papa?" Mala said to Joselin as she turned to look up over the desk and confirm.

"That's right, my poppet," her father assured her.

"Then I look forward to it, milady," Ciardis said as she dipped a teasing curtsy to Mala. Mala grinned, delighted.

Ciardis bid good day to Mala, her father, and the two binders, then exited the shop to return to the Guild. She needed to get back and do Stephanie's laundry for the week.

***

The next morning, she woke to a small message glowing in her *tobama* ball, a small, crystalline orb that held notices, and, in this case, voice messages from mages. Yawning slightly, she raised her hand and tapped the glowing orb that sat by her bedside. Knowing she'd be able to hear the message even from across the room, she stumbled over to the armoire to grab a simple dress to slip on. Damias's voice came echoing out.

"Ciardis, wear pants and a tunic...and bring coffee."

He sounded irritated, she thought with a light grin. If there was anyone worse than her at getting up in the mornings, it had to be Damias. Taking off the dress she'd just put on, she rang the bell to the kitchens and asked for a tray of coffee to be brought to her room. As she struggled with tugging the tunic over her head, she realized that she had no idea where the meeting was supposed to be held. Then a knock sounded at her door. She shouted a quick, "Come in!" as she fussed with the ties on her bell sleeves.

Terris peeked her head in and then hurried over to her struggling friend. After they'd settled the ties, she said eagerly, "Our interviews will be held together!"

Ciardis looked at her with wide eyes. Terris giggled, knowing instantly what the look was for, and said, "I *know*, right? Vana and Serena in the same room? It's going to be something to see!"

Ciardis rolled her eyes. "I think that's something I could do without seeing. You were there when they had that out-and-out screaming match at dance rehearsal."

Terris shuddered. "And to think, recruits are warned against embarrassing their sponsors. Really, it should be the other way around. Hopefully this time will be less...public."

"As if," muttered Ciardis as she grabbed some of her books. "I think the whole city block heard that last fight."

At that moment, a second knock came at the door, with a chime to indicate it was the household staff. Terris went to open it with Ciardis close behind her, hoping it was the coffee. It was. Grabbing the carafe from one young maid, Ciardis told her thanks, as the girl curtsied in return. To Terris, Ciardis said, "I hope you know where the interviews are supposed to be held."

"Yep," replied her friend, as she took a fruit and breadbasket from a second maid's hands.

They hurried to an upper floor, and Ciardis grinned when she realized they were going into the tower. The top of the tower was a beautiful atrium with glass windows that opened on all sides to the fresh sea air. She was happy the meeting was being held there as she hated being crammed into windowless, hot rooms.

As they arrived, they saw that none of the others had arrived yet. *No surprise there*, thought Ciardis. *Damias must have messaged me from his room.*

She and Terris busied themselves unpacking the fruit, jams, and bread from the basket while they set the coffee down. A few minutes later, to their relief, Serena, Damias, and two other women arrived. When they were all settled in around the round table in the center of the room, Damias cleared his throat—after gulping half his mug of coffee, of course. "Ciardis, may I present to you Lady Vana, the sponsor of Terris, and Mary Windstorm, Terris's tutorials instructor."

Ciardis nodded, trying to swallow a small bit of bread stuck in her throat. Terris discreetly passed her a glass of water before she started choking, and Damias gracefully moved on. "Terris, I am Damias Firelancer, Ciardis's instructor. This is Lady Serena, her sponsor."

Terris nodded. Ciardis had finally gotten herself under control, though not without a withering glare from Serena. Terris, sitting beside her, kicked her foot under the table in solidarity.

"Well," drawled Vana, "It's a pleasure to finally meet you, Ciardis. The first Weathervane to be chosen in decades…how *special*."

Ciardis gave her a tight smile, catching the disdain in her tone.

Serena raised her glass. "To our girls!"

Damias, Vana, and Mary completed the toast with varying degrees of enthusiasm.

Half an hour later, Ciardis was miserable. The bickering had started the moment the toast had ended. Ciardis had hoped the interview process would begin immediately but the sponsors and tutorials instructors seemed to be leisurely munching on breakfast and making small talk in advance. Pleasantries had gone out the door when Serena had commented—or sniped, rather on the topic of Vana's poorly dyed hair.

Once, Mary had had to physically hold Vana back from slapping Serena over some insult, and Damias looked like he had a headache from the constant abuse flying around. Apparently deciding that he'd had enough, Damias rapped a small fork against his glass of water, signifying an end to the petty snipes between the two warring parties. "Let's just get on with it," he growled.

"Fine." Clearing her throat, Lady Vana said, "As we all know, Chimaeran girls are famed for their ability to communicate with any other species."

"Just the girls?" whispered Ciardis to Terris. It wasn't as if either of the two sponsors was paying them any attention, anyway.

"The boys can change into any animal form, magical or mundane," Terris quickly whispered back.

"Vana," said Damias in a warning tone. He had noted that she'd gone back to a glaring contest with Serena.

"Which is why," Vana hastily continued as she turned from glaring at her nemesis, "we're here not to discuss your promotion to trainee level but the preparations for your patron hunt and the future use of your magical talents during the Hunt."

"Yes," said Serena, seemingly determined that Vana would not have the floor for long. "As I told Ciardis when she arrived, her extraordinary talents mean an automatic conferral of trainee status."

Damias looked at Mary and tilted his head to her indicating that she had the floor.

Mary smiled, looking at Terris and Ciardis. "Since both of you

 68

have already been accepted as trainees, now we'd like to discuss your Patron candidates."

Both Ciardis and Terris sat up straight at that. This was definitely new.

CHAPTER SEVEN

"But before we do we need to be certain of your abilities, which is why we asked you to come today," Damias said.

He stood and waved his hand at the doorway, as if inviting someone to come in. They all stood and watched as the double doors swung inward, revealing two armed men with swords strapped across their backs and small, covered cages in each hand.

Ciardis eyed the cages warily. This did *not* look like it was going to be a friendly and relaxed guidance session. The two men set down the cages at their feet, bowed, and retired to one side of the atrium.

Their group rose from the table and approached the four cages, Terris and Ciardis trailing behind the others uncertainly. Ciardis was sure from the look on Terris's face that she had no idea what was going to happen either.

Damias stopped in front of the two cages on the left and turned to the group. He addressed Ciardis and Terris. "These are *Rabiae*, woodland creatures that eat and absorb magic."

Ciardis frowned; she had heard of the innocent-looking little beasts. They were favored hunting targets of the nobility who lived on estates near Vaneis. The nobles, many of them from the bloodlines of mages, had delighted in facing the magical threat of the *Rabiae*. They ran the little animals down on horseback and speared them. The problem was that once speared, the *Rabiae* emitted a foul purple stench that clung to clothes for days. Ciardis had spent many a day scrubbing fabric clean of the rank odor, which never deadened the olfactory sense as most bad smells did.

"The *Rabiae* are a byproduct of the Initiate Wars of over two centuries ago," Damias said. "They were designed by manipulative mages to appeal to children."

Vana and Serena shuddered delicately, and Vana said, "With those cute floppy ears and soft fur, many young mages come across them and keep them as pets. These 'pets' slowly steal every drop of power these children have. The mage children who retain them as pets then become mundane."

"It is for reasons like this that certain categories of mage work have been restricted, and must be approved by Imperial mandate before commencing," said Mary. "But the Rabiae have already been created, and are impossible to eradicate with magic. As such, we've done our best to make practical use of their kind."

"Today, you will each pick one up, but for no more than a few minutes. The Rabiae not only absorb magic; they also memorize which talent each person exhibits," continued Damias. "Once collected, their memories of such characteristics were used by their masters to catalogue the bloodlines of mages that would useful." He snorted, "It was barbaric then, and it's barbaric now, to consider breeding in order to ensure a magical bloodline is produced."

Ciardis frowned, not because she disagreed, but because she was wondering, *isn't that what the nobles do, anyway? Only marry other nobles, just as mages only marry other mages?*

Vana summoned the two trainers from their corners. The men wore tight leather jerkins, the hilts of their swords jutting upward. They looked powerful, like the mercenaries Ciardis had sometimes seen on the roads up north. Opening the cages, they dragged the *Rabiae* out by the nape of their neck. Ciardis couldn't help but think that the trainers appeared as if they were prepared to exert more force than was needed, even though she knew what the beasts were capable of. These two big, strapping men each held a *Rabiae* in one hand by the loose, soft skin at the nape of its neck. The *Rabiae* hung unresisting in their grip. Their soft thumper legs kicked lightly and their noses twitched, but they made no noise. Ciardis smiled grimly, thinking, *No wonder children like them so much.*

The men approached the two young women as the adults moved back into a half circle behind Terris and Ciardis. The two young women exchanged nervous glances and simultaneously reached forward for the bundles of gray fur.

From a pocket, Damias produced a large, round timer and began a three-minute countdown. After the three minutes were up, Ciardis and Terris gave the *Rabiae* back to the trainers, who clapped metal braces on their small necks and attached the braces to metal studs in the floor. They weren't going anywhere.

With a glance at Damias, Lady Serena stepped forward. She began to conjure, her hands lightly resting over the fur of the two *Rabiae*. From those small forms arose a shimmering light. Ciardis's *Rabiae*, on the left, was red; the *Rabiae* on the right, Terris's, was blue. The swirls of color condensed, but not into any shape or form. Ciardis thought they looked like snow clouds.

Serena said, "Those swirling colors represent your magical cores. I should be able to read them – to see an image that represents the essence of your magical potential but the projection is unstable."

"Well, then," said Vana slowly, after Mary prodded her with a swift kick to the shin. "Let me see if I can help."

Terris's eyes twitched in amusement, but otherwise her face betrayed no emotion. She knew that her sponsor delighted in showing off in front of Serena.

Vana stepped forward and raised her hand to hover over the back of the *Rabiae*. She stood parallel to Serena's still form which had white light from her wrist to the tips of her fingers. Soon Vana's hand began glowing as well. Vana tapped into her mage core slowly, not wanting to withdraw too much magic, too fast. A purple orb rose from the palm of her hand to the center of the swirling blue and red clouds above the *Rabiae*. When Damias saw Ciardis's questioning look, he said, "Vana Cloudbreaker is an Initiate of the Unknown from the Madrassa, and is occasionally seconded to the Imperial Army for assignments."

Ciardis's eyes widened at the mention of the school. Even she knew of the fabled Madrassa, also known as "the Red Madrassa," due to the brilliantly colored year-round foliage on the campus trees. It was the Empire's premiere school of magic for young mages. *Young, rich mages,* she thought with no little bitterness. It took a few more seconds before she internalized the fact that Damias had basically just told her that Vana was a Spy for the Imperial Army…or, at the very least, a part of its Special Operations division. Ciardis thought about Vana with more respect after that.

It looked like the two sponsors were making some headway with the cloud. The small purple orb from Vana's hands had grown to envelope the two clouds in front of Serena. Out of the mist, words formed. Ciardis narrowed her eyes; the words were written in the fluid squiggles of the Sahalian language, but made no sense. Wasn't she supposed to know this language already?

Terris whispered in her ear, "You have to relax the first time you use a newly transferred ability. Just like you did when Stephanie copied the skill of reading to you. Take a small breath and *relax.*"

Slowly, Ciardis let her stiff shoulders loosen and the knot in her stomach unraveled. The Sahalian squiggles shifted into the Common Tongue before her eyes. The text was only two sentences long.

One will have the power to rend the Empire asunder. The other will shift to the kith's side in their dire hour.

There was silence around the circle as they all took in the rather cryptic message. At last, Mary Windstorm asked, "Are they supposed to be that...*vague?*"

"No," replied Serena as she bit her lip. "In fact, these fur balls aren't supposed to be prophetic at all." She looked like she was about to kick one of the fur balls in question.

Damias said brightly, "Well, at least they've confirmed that our girls have gifts—otherwise, the Rabiae wouldn't have interacted with them."

Vana gave an unladylike snort. "We knew that before we hired these fur balls and their trainers at four hundred shillings an hour."

Damias shot her an irritated look and then sighed as he rubbed his hands over his eyes. "Okay, let's discuss this later." He motioned for the trainers to re-cage the beasts.

Terris, Ciardis, Damias, Serena, Vana and Mary moved to sit back down at the table. With a last lingering glance at the other two cages which sat near the *Rabiae's* blanketed ones, Ciardis followed and sat down. She was wondering what was in them.

"Now the real fun begins," Vana said primly. "Bring the *Cardiara!*"

The second set of cages was opened to reveal glass jars. In each jar was a small figure that emitted green sparks as it fluttered around its container. When the jars were deposited in the center of the table Serena folded her hands, "We apologize for the accommodations, milord and milady. We would ask for your sign of honor before proceeding with the agreement."

The fey folded their arms in haughty disdain. Then the one on the left, the male, raised a finger and slowly traced out a large glyph on the interior surface of the glass jar. The female gave him a disapproving look, but said nothing.

The glyph glowed brightly, and the adults around the table smiled in approval. Upon seeing this Serena directed her smile at the male fey, "Thank you sir, and welcome to the Companions' Guild."

She reached forward and unfastened the lid on the male's jar. He slowly floated out and settled on the tabletop. The trainers removed his empty jar and his companion's from sight with her still inside. Damias said to the little man, "In return for your sign and honest opinion, we will free you into the Forest of Ameles, as you have requested."

The fey nodded curtly. "I am Mainar. Who would you have me assess?"

Damias nodded to the two girls who sat across from him at the table.

"Before you begin," said Serena, "we would like to magically record this statement on a *tobama* ball." The male Cardiara nodded his acceptance, turned, and narrowed his eyes as he took in Terris and Ciardis in turn.

Serena slipped a small tobama ball from her pocket and held it over the table in the palm of her hand. The translucent glass darkened to an opaque mist, indicating that it was recording the proceedings.

"The one on the left is one of your bloody Weathervanes," Mainar said sharply. "She has inherited her mother's power for enhancement and her father's gift for calculation. The one on the right is a shifter of the Chimaera, able to temporarily assume any form she chooses."

Sighs of relief echoed around the table. Nodding to Mainar, Serena said, "We thank you for your grace and wisdom in this matter." She signaled for the trainers to escort him out.

Once they were alone, Mary said, "Well! This is excellent news, girls, and your prospective Patrons will be pleased."

Vana added, "The words of the Cardiara have been used as binding contracts since before the Initiate Wars." With grudging acknowledgement of Serena's gifts, Vana continued, "As a project Companion Serena will be able to project Mainar's announcement of your gifts to a conclave of prospective patrons."

Damias and Mary then reached into their pockets for a folded sheet of paper. Damias deferred to Mary, saying, "Milady, if you please."

A small smile graced Mary's thin face as she leaned forward with eagerness. "Terris, four of the finest lords in the city of Sandrin have already petitioned for the right to your contract."

"These four are among the select few we considered most worthy of your talents," said Vana. "They will be given favorable position to impress upon you their merits at the dance and initial presentation."

"But remember this is *your* choice," Mary said. "We will advise you upon who we think are the best candidates financially, politically, and aesthetically, but it is you who must make the final decision."

Damias said, "Yes. Make no mistake: the dancing, the Practicals, and the pretty gowns are fabulous. But you will sign a binding contract with this person. They will care for you as their own. After all, even in the dissolution of a contract, companions are entitled to monthly payments for life."

Each of the sponsors and tutorials were looking with seriousness at Ciardis and Terris to impress upon them the gravity of becoming a companion.

With a sharp nod, Mary Windstorm continued, "Terris, your prospective patrons are Lord Kerrin of Nardes, Prince Heir Simeon of Sandrin, Viscount Derek of Mutlin, and Lord Varo of Sandrin."

"In preparation for the Patron Hunt you'll be given a binder detailing each Patron's family history, their lands, their wealth, and their persona," said Vana smoothly. "You are expected to give this information your full consideration."

"Of course, Lady Vana," replied Terris, her eyes downcast.

"Ciardis, your considerable talents have attracted the interest of six candidates," said Damias. She blinked in surprise upon hearing the number.

"Any of whom we'd be proud to welcome as Patrons to the Companions' Guild," said Serena.

"These candidates are the Viscount Iskas of Marce," began Damias.

"A *minor* noble of little repute," Vera interjected.

"A minor noble with *wealthy* coffers," rebutted Serena.

"Ladies, please," Damias said. "The others are General Barnaren of Principas Vale, Initiate Soundsoar of the Madrassa, Princess Heir Marissa of Sandrin, and Archduke Clarin of Vaneis—"

At the announcement of the Archduke's name, Terris grasped Ciardis's hands in excitement and gasped aloud. Ciardis returned her grin and looked back to Damias to hear the last name.

Damias smiled, aware that the Archduke hailed from Ciardis's home province. He continued, "And Lord Mage Meres Kinsight."

Ciardis's mind was awhirl with what she already knew about her prospective Patrons, and she felt certain that Terris was no less preoccupied.

"For both of you," continued Serena, "we have drafted an announcement to be delivered at the conclave of prospective Patrons in two weeks."

Serena cleared her throat and began reading from a piece of paper.

"On behalf of the Companions' Guild, we welcome you, milords and ladies, to the conclave on behalf of Ciardis Weathervane and

Terris Kithwalker."

Ciardis and Terris looked at each other with raised eyebrows at their new titles, but declined to interrupt.

"This is an auspicious occasion, as we plan for the debut of two of our finest companion trainees as they come of age. Participants in the Patron Hunt of the two aforementioned candidates will be housed in the Duke of Carne's villa off the palace grounds. We look forward to your attendance in celebration of these young women, whom we are proud to call our own."

"That is all for today," said Vana while she glanced at the position of the mid-afternoon sun. "You are both to spend the remaining six weeks studying those binders day and night in preparation."

"Though, of course," said Mary Windstorm, "you are also expected to continue your work on your tutorials, as well."

The two young women nodded, took the binders, and exited quickly.

CHAPTER EIGHT

Ciardis had very few days off from her tutorials instructions with Damias and Lady Serena. With the start of the Patron Hunt only days away they had been adamant about practicing as much as possible. Even with her time off from tutorials she still had to study the history and backgrounds of her potential suitors. So today she sat in the library, her head resting on the palm of her hand as she traced the letters on the page, occasionally glancing at the dictionary next to her to check the definition of a particularly difficult word.

This time she was studying the history and exploits of General Barnaren's kin. A militaristic family from Principas Vale—a region to the west of Sandrin known for its many olive groves—his family had led many Imperial military campaigns, including the small skirmishes now being fought in the North.

Ciardis smiled as she looked at the portrait of his face while focusing on the hard, chiseled angles and stormy gray eyes. He was older than her other candidates, with more than twenty years on her, but she wouldn't expect anything less of the Commanding General of the Imperial Army. His powers lay in fire conjuring, and Lord Cannon, Lady Serena's Patron, was his second-in-command. General Barnaren had been known to call giant red wolves of fire to his side in battle.

She continued reading, wondering why he had not yet taken a wife; at age thirty-seven, it was prudent for him to have a family and secure an heir considering the large tracts of land his family commanded in Principas Vale. Then she turned the page and saw that he *had* been married, to a healer of great skill. She had died in battle at Marin Ridge.

Beneath this text was a little pocket containing a note, emblazoned with the inscription, *"For the eyes of the Companions' Guild only."*

Curious, she opened it, rationalizing that if it was in the binder, it must be for her.

From Sarah, Head Archivist, Companions' Guild
In efforts to prepare Companion Trainee Ciardis Weathervane (née Vane until assumption of her 18th Birthday and approval from the Talents Guild) I have spoken to the head archivist of the family of Principas Vale.

General Barnaren is not only in search of a companion, but also a wife, one who will bear him at least one child, of either sex, within a three-year period. This is to assure the security of his line and the succession of his mage spirit's path in the event of his death in battle.

With these stipulations, if Ciardis will consider him as a Prospective Patron, she must be prepared to undergo a full health screening and fertility assessment by a Sahalian midwife.

A second note on a separate sheet followed.

Arten Simas, Principas Vale Archivist
Upon successful birth of the first child, the companion of
General Barnaren will be granted the status an annual stipend
of five times the initial stipend agreement, lands of her
choosing in Principas Vale and the freedom to marry a suitable
partner of her choosing.

Ciardis sat back to think. There was much to consider here. From what she knew it was rare for a companion to marry anyone other than their Patron, if they chose to marry at all. She needed to think about all the responsibilities she'd assume as a Wife and Lady of a manor, or even multiple manors in an area as large as a Vale, and she knew that her enhancement powers would be needed by her Patron in various capacities. However, before beginning her study of the Patron binders, she had not considered childbirth. At least, not until she was older - much older. She frowned, deciding to discuss the matter with Lady Serena at a later date, and stood, stretching her arms wide. She'd been in the library all morning.

To her surprise, just as she stood, around the corner came Lady Sarah. "Hello, Ciardis," said Sarah, whose hair was streaked with bright shades of green.

Ciardis murmured a polite response. Sarah turned to look over the pile of documents that sat on the library table—family charts going back many generations, binders of prospective Patrons, analects of the famous Mages of the Madrassa, and histories of the noble families of Sandrin, Principas, and Vaneis. She gave Ciardis a wry smile as she said, "I remember the long nights of studying for my choice. Ream upon ream of birthdates, deaths, and family patronage." She shuddered delicately.

Ciardis looked at her curiously. "Whom did you ultimately decide upon as your patron?"

Sarah raised an eyebrow and gave her a smile. "I declined them all."

Ciardis gasped, her eyes wide with surprise as she stuttered, "W-why?"

"I already had the best job in the world, and none of the libraries of my prospective Patrons could hold a candle to this one," Sarah swept her hand out to indicate the large and beautiful multi-floor library. It was built largely of maple, all varnished to a mellow shine. "How could I give this up?" she asked almost to herself.

Ciardis stared, wondering if she would ever find anything that she loved as much as Sarah did her chosen profession. Perhaps...

"Now, enough of this sentimental reminiscing! Pack up your things and come with me. Quickly, quickly," Sarah added. Ciardis did as she was told, and she soon had two scrolls stuffed under one arm and a satchel strapped across her back that was filled with books.

As they left the library, Sarah said, "Tonight is your eighteenth birthday, and you have less than two weeks before your Patron Hunt."

Ciardis nodded with a gulp. She'd been trying not to think about that. She said, "Yes, milady," as they dodged servant girls. The girls were rushing in multiple directions – arms filled with flower arrangements, huge bundles of pretty fabric, and what looked suspiciously like a very tall cake.

Sarah nodded, then pulled a small round orb out of her dress pocket as they entered a square room on the other side of the palace. "This is the Memory Room. It was used by Imperial Consorts to lock in the memories of young princes and princesses as they transitioned from childhood to adulthood," Sarah paused. "There is a different room for the memories of reigning monarchs."

As they entered the empty room, the door clanged shut behind them. Ciardis saw that the entire room was decorated in midnight blue, with pale geometric designs etched onto the surfaces of every wall. No furniture was in the room, and Ciardis' skirt raised no dust as they walked to the center of the room. Upon reaching the middle Ciardis noted a small depression in the floor, which Sarah and then Ciardis knelt before.

"In my hands, I hold a memory ball," Sarah told Ciardis. "It records memories from participants, and keeps them safe for future use." She set the memory ball in the depression. "Each mage family, including yours keeps a memory ball to imprint ancestral transitions and convey the descendant's transition to their powers," Sarah explained while looking down at the orb. "Only those with a sympathetic touch can activate a memory ball, and we can only store new memories in conjunction with a projector such as Serena."

She smiled at Ciardis. "Several of our mage families have left their memory balls in the Guild's care as they have died out, or for safekeeping." She touched the still orb before them. "This is the memory ball of the Weathervane family." With a regretful sigh, Sarah continued, "Because of the way the memories are transferred to the memory balls, once stored, only a descendant can view them."

They both stood and Sarah straightened out her skirts. "As such, I will leave you to learn about your inherent powers. Your powers should arrive on the midnight bell of the morrow, the first day of your eighteenth year."

Sarah continued, "Of course, that's usually true of skill sets that are non-elemental in origin."

"Non-elemental?" questioned Ciardis.

"Powers that are restricted to one talent. Some children develop talents over the elements, such as wind and fire or even healing, which requires training from a very young age, instead of one skill," said Sarah.

83

Ciardis had the slight suspicion that Sarah didn't approve of such powers.

Probably thinks they'd burn her library down around her, she thought.

Sarah put a finger to her lips in thought. "Weathervane heritage has always been unpredictable, though."

"What should I expect?" Ciardis asked, a little worried.

With a frown, Sarah said, "The transition may be uncomfortable, but I can't say for sure. Transitions are specific to each mage family. After I leave, you'll be able to activate the memory ball due your blood right. The room itself will act as a conduit and a power source."

Sarah waved her hand and suddenly a door appeared in the wall to their right. "To make sure the overnight adjustment to your talents goes well, you will stay in the bedroom beyond that door. I'll make sure a maid brings you meals, and Serena will come to you tomorrow to test your skills. Any questions?"

Ciardis did a slight curtsy, and said, "No." She couldn't think of anything else to say.

With that, Sarah swept out of the room, locking the door behind her.

Ciardis contemplated the silvery orb in the depression for a long moment. Then, deciding it was now or never—she'd been waiting months for the off chance that her powers would come in after all—she nicked her finger with a hairpin. She carefully lowered her bleeding finger to tap the ball's gleaming surface and then watched with wide eyes as the silver absorbed the liquid, leaving no trace of red on its surface.

At first, nothing seemed to happen, and she had time to wonder if she should squeeze out a larger dollop of her lifeblood, but suddenly, a humming sound began to fill the room. It grew louder and louder as the orb rose slowly into the air. Streaks of blue lightning sizzled down from the ceiling and rose from the floor to meet the orb's glimmering exterior.

Ciardis stumbled back hastily, almost tripping on her own skirt. The humming had stopped, but the orb crackled with live fire across its surface. She frowned. "What am I supposed to do now?"

There was no answer from the pulsing lightning and arcing fire in the center of the room. Ciardis looked around hoping for a manual or display to pop up somewhere.

Maybe the geometric symbols on the walls will rearrange themselves into words?

She'd meant the thought sarcastically, but she wasn't too far off. Half a second later, a bright beam of blue light shot out of the memory ball and struck the center of the wall opposite her.

It was so bright that Ciardis had to shade her eyes as she squinted. The light formed a shimmering square box. As she watched, the symbols on the wall began to fade slowly into the stone. She gasped at what she saw taking the symbols' place.

Moving images of people were beginning to form on the wall.

The images of people, as vibrant and colorful as a living person, changed frequently. She saw the graceful figure of a woman dancing in a ballroom, and next, a charging swordsman on a field. Both bore the distinct golden eyes of the Weathervanes. The memory ball flowed from scene to scene as each ancestor gained powers. Many appeared to do so long after their eighteenth birthdays had passed from the lines and age that appeared on their faces.

She saw a woman in a *stolla*, a long flowing dress which tied at the nape of neck, playing with a child near the sea. The woman suddenly crumpled to her knees with her hands splayed in the sand. Her eyes glowed with a yellow as bright as the sun for a few moments, and Ciardis knew that, just like the others, she had transitioned into her powers.

When the next scene appeared, Ciardis walked over to the wall, trying to touch the moving image that looked so real, though it was flat. *It's not the same as Sarah's multi-dimensional projections,* she thought, *but it is beautiful.*

As she touched the wall it rippled with light, bending away from her finger like small waves in a lake after you skip a rock. She heard another sound coming from the orb behind her and turned quickly to investigate, but before she completed the movement, she was hit with a wave of light and sound so all-encompassing that she fainted.

As she lay on the floor, she dreamed. She dreamed of every ancestor who'd accessed the Weathervane memory ball, and knew their thoughts, their exploits, their dreams, and their histories. When she'd gone through each ancestor's transition memories, her mind went blank. She drifted in a black aether, nothing before her or around her until she started falling.

When she woke, she felt dirt under her finger tips and a breeze wafting through the air. She opened her eyes, and there stood the woman she'd seen on the beach who'd been playing with the child. Her ancestor. Then Ciardis noticed where she was—or, rather, where she was not.

She was no longer in the room she'd been in earlier. The landscape was flat, dark, and foreboding. It stretched on for miles in either direction with no trees or buildings in sight, just gently waving grass. *Even my clothes are different,* she realized in shock. She hesitantly touched the loose stolla of the clans, which had replaced the formal day gown she had been wearing.

The woman laughed gently as Ciardis's cautious eyes turned back to her. "You should not fear me, daughter," she said. "I am your many times great-grandmother, Artis."

Ciardis trembled, but said, "My…my name is Ciardis."

The other woman's laughter bubbled up again. "Which means

'Daughter of Artis' in the Old Tongue! How appropriate!" She clapped her hands, delighted.

Smiling widely, Ciardis curtsied. She hadn't known that. "Where are we, then, Lady Artis?"

Artis raised her arm to indicate the vast plains. "We are in a memory—a memory of my early life, before I joined the clan of my husband and changed all that I knew. But more importantly, we are in your mind. You have opened the ancestral memory ball."

Ciardis licked her lips. "I have. I have been taken in by the Companions' Guild. My Patron Hunt is in two weeks, and I have yet to access my powers."

Artis nodded. "It is the way of our women. Although, it is not always our path to be a lord's bound companion," she continued with a teasing smile. "I was—*am*—Warrior Leader for my clan, as well as Consort."

Ciardis raised her chin, determined not to be cowed. "That may be so, milady, and I hope to achieve such a rank one day. But I grew up poor and orphaned, often without food, and with little privacy."

Artis sighed. "Yes, your childhood was unfortunate...and it is your decision to move forward. But we have little time left. You have viewed the transition memories of your ancestors, yes?"

"Indeed I have," replied Ciardis, meeting her eyes.

"Good," Artis replied. "Now, realize that they are but memories—no more, no less. But some of the visions might come in handy in the future." She extended both her hands towards Ciardis, palms up. "Place your palms in mine."

When their skin touched, it was as if their two minds became one. Ciardis could feel Artis flitting through her mind, tugging on core memories. When she questioned her, all she got was a gruff, "This will strengthen your defenses when the time comes."

Ciardi saw how her ancestors would use their power of

enhancement to tap into the mage cores of their chosen partners. On the battlefield they presented formidable foes – not only increasing the power of the other person's magic but allowing them to fine tune their attacks. Ciardis saw an orb of battle fire held until the precise moment and then flung at the target with such force and power that it eliminated a legion upon impact. In another vision, she saw a companion enhance the soft and subtle lilt of a musician's voice as it soared over a dinner party at an elegant townhome.

After a long while, Artis said in a tired whisper, "There, my dear. I've unlocked your gift. I can't do any more tonight. Come back for lessons, yes?"

Her voice grew softer with each passing word, until she had disappeared from the landscape, and Ciardis drifted away, as well.

***

Hours later, Ciardis awakened on the cold stone floor.

She groaned at the ache in her head. Lifting her fingers tentatively, she touched a stream of liquid running down the curve of her cheek. Bringing her fingertips to her eyes, she squinted and then stared in horror at what was clearly blood. She traced the path to her earlobe. She'd bled from her ears at some point.

As she rose steadily, she felt…alive. Her whole body was a-stir with energy. She could even see blue lightning streaks zapping through the walls all around her.

Across from her, a doorway appeared—or, rather, a section of the wall outlined in white disappeared. On the other side of the new opening was a four-poster bed in a small room. Stumbling towards it, she saw a washbasin on a corner pedestal with fresh water and a small bundle on the bed. Ciardis grimaced as she entered the room; her eyes were playing funny tricks on her. She kept seeing glimmers of light shining out of the corners of her eyes, and whenever she looked directly at an object, it blazed with power.

Even the plain porcelain washbasin glittered. She wasn't sure she wanted to stick her hands into the water, but her disgust with the blood dripping down her face won the contest. As she wiped her face with the towel beside the basin, she saw the bloody water that she'd squeezed into the bowl magically clear itself. Fresh water appeared without a drop of red to mar its surface. Handy, that.

After moving over to the bed, she picked up a note that sat beside a cloth-wrapped bundle.

> *The first experience with new mage powers can be unsettling. For a few hours you will be seeing the mage spells tied into each object and person around you. The sensation will soon fade.*
>
> *Rest well and welcome to your powers.*
> *- The Companions Council*

Putting the note aside, she turned to the cloth-wrapped bundle. Inside, she discovered a small, golden ankle bracelet. She handled it gingerly. The bracelet, with its intricate links and delicate moonstone and sapphire gems, was probably worth more than she would make in a year once she'd signed her contract. On the bed beside the bracelet lay a note.

> *Ciardis, this is a gift from one of your prospective patrons upon a successful transition. Your first gift! Treat it with significance.—*
> *Serena.*

Then Serena's handwriting disappeared, and different handwriting ghosted in to replace it.

*You hold a moonstone and sapphire bracelet. It will allow you
to transfer your mind and body into the Aether Realm between
the mundane world and the heavens. May your journey be
fair.*

Scratch that, Ciardis thought ruefully. *It's worth ten times what I'll
make in my best year—any jewelry with a connection to the Aether Realm
is.* She knew from reading the biographies of her patrons that two of
them had the means to casually purchase such a trinket for a stranger,
two had the magical skills to create such a bracelet, and one had both
the means and magic to do it himself. She wondered which one it
was—the successful viscount or the general?

She sat down and thought about the Aether Realm itself. It wasn't
truly another realm in the sense of the Gods' Heaven; it was merely
a plane of existence that could be accessed only by mages. It was said
to be a battlefield of magical games and untold mysteries. Ciardis
sniffed with disdain. She had enough mystery going on just picking
out the patron she'd spend the rest of her life with! She didn't need
magical games added on top of that.

But then, the man had paid a considerable sum, magical or coin,
to get this bracelet for her. *Although it could also be Princess Heir
Marissa,* thought Ciardis with some dismay. She had no problem
with women per say, she just didn't know how to court one. *Maybe
she's looking for a strictly platonic relationship?*

Either way whichever patron it turned out to be would expect her
to greet them properly and thank them for the gift. And there was
only one way to do that. She knew it would be perceived as a personal
insult to the Patron if she didn't wear the bracelet and meet that
person or their representative in the Aether. Finally, she shrugged,
thinking with sarcasm, *some people take their intended on pleasant river
cruises; the nobility of Sandrin take you on potentially dangerous trips to*

an invisible realm.

She shuddered; she was no fool. She knew the bracelet came with a downside. Although pretty to look at, she couldn't control the gemstones. They would deliver her to a programmed location and deposit her back here, if programmed to do so, after a set time. She didn't like walking into something unknown, but in this case, she had to—Serena had made that clear by giving her the bauble. The Aether bracelet had been accepted by the Companions' Guild, and would be treated with respect as a cherished memento. Taking hold of the bracelet, Ciardis sat on the bed, reached down to lift her dress, and slid it on over her ankle.

For a moment, nothing happened…and then she was once more engulfed in darkness.

CHAPTER NINE

This time when she awoke, it felt like more than just the visions that had come with activating the memory ball. This time it was as if her body had been transported alongside her mind, into the Aether realm. In fact, she was fairly sure that that was exactly what had happened. She pinched herself; she couldn't believe she was actually here – mind, body and soul. She looked around and sunlight pierced her eyes, streaming down through a fall canopy of changing leaves, clad in the red, gold, and brown of late autumn and early winter. She shivered as she hugged her arms close to her body.

Wherever she was, it wasn't anywhere near Sandrin. She knew that the Aether Realm mimicked the geography of the mundane realm, but this place didn't feel familiar. Judging by the climate and rolling landscape, it lay somewhere between the cold, windswept mountains of Vaneis and the oceans off Sandrin. Great trees rose far above her, and a cold breeze rippled through the air as crisp, colorful leaves trembled and fell to the ground. The courting dress she wore was no protection against the cool weather here.

 92

She turned around and around, looking for another soul. *This is real,* Ciardis thought, *but where is my suitor? Am I supposed to know where to go?* Irritated, she hiked up her dress and shook her foot to wake up the bracelet. She muttered fiercely to it, "You know, I could use some help here. Hello? Wake up, you silly thing. There's no one here. Take me back."

There was no response.

Suddenly, her flesh began to rise in goose bumps; she was being watched. She looked up and saw him. There, on the crest of a nearby hill, stood a young man. He was dressed for a hunt—an expensive one, by the looks of it. A few years younger than she—three would be her best guess—he clutched a crossbow in his hands. His hair was soot-black and his tunic a brilliant green. He kept his eyes focused directly on Ciardis as he approached. He had an arrow drawn into a bow but tilted downward at the moment. He held it tightly, as if he were ready to shoot her at any second.

She noticed that his eyes were as green as his tunic. "You there! Who are you?" he shouted at her as he approached Ciardis. "How did you get here?"

Ciardis scowled at him as he made his way over to her. *What kind of greeting is that?* She thought with disdain, *and who is this foolish boy? Whoever he is, he needs to get lost now. I need to prepare for my Patron.* As she straightened her shoulders and prepared to give the brat a tongue-lashing, she thought with excitement, *I'll bet my Patron is General Barnaren! He must be waiting for me in the glade off to the east. It'll be so romantic. Perhaps he's prepared a picnic for the two of us.*

Turning her mind back to the boy in front of her, she noted with some admiration that he held the weapon with some surety. *He knows how to use it, then,* she thought. Despite the weapon in his hands and his fine clothes, he reminded her of the tanner's boy who'd boasted of a big kill after the autumn hunt two years ago. The whole village

TERAH EDUN

had known it was his mother who'd taken down the stag, but still he
strutted around with a puffed chest and enough bravado to make a
rutting elk wince in embarrassment. Although, the slight tremble in
the boy's arms was a small sign of his anxiety.

Calmly, she said, "I could ask you the same question." To put him
at ease, she continued, careful to leave out certain details, as she didn't
want the boy to know a powerful General was waiting for her. "My
name is Ciardis. I put on an ankle bracelet, and here I am. And you?"

He lifted his bow and pointed it straight at her chest. "It doesn't
matter who I am." He warily lowered the weapon as he said, "Did
you say a bracelet?"

"Yes," she said, exasperated. She lifted up her dress and wiggled
her ankle to show off the pretty ornament fastened to her leg. He
didn't look like he believed her. In fact, she was sure he didn't believe
her, as he had raised the crossbow once more. "You daft-brained
boy," Ciardis scolded. "Don't be so hasty with that weapon. I've told
you what I know."

He didn't lower the bow this time, "That bracelet is a gift that I
entrusted to my senior arms man. Only a Weathervane should have
it."

Ciardis shouted, "I'm the Weathervane, you git! At least, I'm *a*
Weathervane. And if you expect me to believe that you are my
Patron, you are delusional as well as an idiot. There are no boys in
my Hunt, only men."

Quickly she added as she remembered a certain Princess Heir,
"And a woman."

He stared at her, seemingly aghast at her impertinence, and finally
lowered his bow. "Whether or not you believe the bracelet belongs to
me is immaterial," he said arrogantly with a curl of his lip. "I don't
know how you got that bracelet, but rest assured that you are not
who it was intended for."

Ciardis snarled, ready to smack the boy; she wasn't exactly elated with his condescending tone, and was even less so when he muttered to himself, "A fool peasant. I've lost all chance, then."

"Hey, now!" snapped Ciardis. "I may be of common stock, but I'm no fool. And if you weren't so rude, I'd—"

Before she could finish her statement, four men came out of the forest, surrounding Ciardis and the boy on all sides.

Ciardis gasped in astonishment. "Where did they come from?"

More quietly, she conceded, *This Aether Realm is not as empty as I thought it would be.*

Forgetting Ciardis for the moment, the boy turned so that they stood side-by-side, facing the man in front together. The other three had fanned out to box them. The fact that the boy beside her immediately turned his loaded crossbow on the man to the north told her that he was either a deranged idiot who threatened anyone he came across, or that he knew this man. "Mace," the boy beside her snarled.

Yes, he knows him, Ciardis thought. *At least it's not just me he threatens to kill on a moment's notice.*

"My Lord Prince," the young man addressed with a mocking bow. "You should know better than to wander outside the palace grounds alone."

The man to their east snickered, and when Ciardis looked at him, she could see a glint of cruelty on his pudgy face. She wasn't sure she liked this at all.

"And you should know never to show your face where I can shoot it," said the black-haired young man with an aplomb that Ciardis had to give him credit for. He was handling this situation with more composure than she thought such a young boy surrounded on all sides would have. "How did you and your goons get into the Aether Realm?" he demanded.

Mace drawled, "Powerful friends your highness. Friends that don't like *you*."

Sebastian gritted his teeth, "What are you doing here?"

A small and satisfied smile crossed Mace's face.

"Why, we're looking for you, Sebastian." He raised his hands in a mocking gesture, laughing. "What else would we be doing here?"

The man to her left side, at the west point, chimed in, "Truly, Prince Sebastian. You failed the talent tests. It's nothing personal."

"Speak for yourself," said the man behind them. "That snot-nosed brat has been a thorn in my side ever since he joined the Ruling Council in his father's stead."

"Glad to know you adore me so, Barden," Sebastian replied sarcastically without turning around. "Makes me proud, it does." Ciardis glanced at Sebastian, surprised at the banter, but didn't turn around to face Barden behind them.

"Forgive my manners, milady," said Mace as he noticed Ciardis standing by Sebastian's side. "Who do I have the pleasure of encountering in this…gorgeous forest?"

Sebastian, stoic beside her, said nothing, but he did relax a bit. She suspected he'd decided she wasn't a part of the four men's scheme. "None of your business," Ciardis replied, her gaze firm and stone cold.

Laughter sounded all around them, and Barden drawled, "I like a woman with spirit. I'm so going to enjoy breaking you."

"No hard feelings, of course, lass," said Mace. "It's just that once we get rid of dear old Sebastian here, we can't have anyone else, especially a weepy woman, telling tall tales."

"Weepy woman?" she snarled in outrage. "I'll show you a weepy woman."

Ciardis pulled a jeweled dagger from her sleeve. Sebastian glanced at her askance, mildly impressed.

"I wouldn't do that if I were you," he said under his breath.

"Mind your business," she snapped. "He didn't insult you."

The man in front of her snorted and pulled out a full-length sword...*from the air.*

"What is it they say on the streets, lass?" he asked. "Ah, yes: 'Bring it on.'"

"What is your business here in the Aether?" she demanded. "And why do you accost us here? Surely four men against one boy and a woman is entirely unfair."

"We live in the Court of Sandrin," said the man standing to the east. "You learn to be pragmatic. If he dies today, our problem disappears."

"On this I agree with Dar," said Barden. "Whatever is necessary to restore our rightful power and connection to the lands...even killing a Prince."

"If you'd actually paid attention in our tutorial lessons you'd know that my death would only make your power dissipate faster." Sebastian said in a voice dripping with venom, "I am the Prince, the heir, the only one who can see the courts through this crisis."

"On the contrary, Sebastian," said Mace as he leaned forward, arms crossed on the hilt of the sword anchored casually in the ground. "We believe—we *know*—that your death is the solution we seek. Life will once more flow throughout the Empire of Algardis. Whether or not a direct descendant of the Algardis Emperor rules is no longer a concern. We need new blood, new power—and a new ruler."

Ciardis was beginning to panic. She did not like where this was going. *A new ruler? The Empire already has an Emperor,* she thought frantically as she edged closer to Sebastian. *They can't possibly be considering assassinating the Emperor!*

As she wracked her brain for a reasonable explanation, she remembered something with dread. According to the court's Trial by

Combat rules, they could get rid of a Prince Heir—and right now, there was only one.

The full impact of that thought hit her with the weight of a ton of bricks. With an internal groan, she thought in horror, *The Prince Heir is a young prince. I'm standing next to a boy claiming to be that prince.*

Perhaps she should have been slightly more polite to him.

***

Sebastian could feel the disturbed thoughts emanating from the girl, but he was more concerned with the mechanics of his upcoming fight. Perhaps he was a weakling when it came to magical talent, but he wasn't completely inept at martial arts. He couldn't depend on the girl; he had no idea who she really was, or if she could fight magically or physically in the Aether Realm. He thought grimly, *if I fire this arrow at Mace, at least I'll have the satisfaction of seeing him meet his death before I meet mine.*

Then Sebastian frowned. His mage core was pulsing erratically, jumping around as if it were itching to be let loose. That had never happened to him before. His magic was essentially dormant. *What could it possibly be responding to?* He wondered with a fascination he really didn't have time for.

Keeping his gaze focused outward, he inwardly sought out the spike of power, diving down to his mage core. He was surprised— *very* surprised—at what he found. The brilliant orange ball of fire that pulsed with his magic was tightly locked down, as always, but it was *rippling*. As he watched, he saw flares coming off of the core, reaching for the tangled flares of another mage core that was hovering in a person right next to him.

It was the power of Ciardis Weathervane.

So she hadn't been lying! To say he was delighted to see his magic

 98

combining with—no, *feeding off of*—the mage core of the girl beside him was an understatement. Assessing his suddenly revived magical talent, he realized that he had enough power to activate the spells to return from the Aether realm. If he'd been deposited to the place in the Aether Realm where he thought he was, then with Ciardis' help all he had to do was cast the enchantment to return home. Unlike some areas in Aether, the jump was relatively easy; here no portals were necessary.

He had just made up his mind when he saw that all four men had decided to pull their weapons from the holders and Mace was bringing up his sword in a firm grip. Sebastian grabbed the girl by her arm, muttered the enchantment, and they disappeared in a whirl of magic.

***

They landed in an opulent apartment the likes of which Ciardis had never seen. She walked forward across a priceless Sahalian rug and turned to find that the men were gone and the boy was staring at her. "What?" she said. "Still want to kill me?"

"Hardly." His head tilted back in surprise as he let out a laugh. "I suppose I do owe you a bit of explanation, Mistress Weathervane," he said ruefully.

She nodded sharply, crossing her arms as she said, "So, you're the future Emperor. Why were those men after you?"

He cast a wry glance in her direction as he walked over to a decanter on a shelf. "Why *wouldn't* they be after me?" He busied himself pouring water from the decanter into the matching crystal glasses by its side. He walked back over and handed her a glass. "They hate me and everything I stand for."

"And what would that be?" Ciardis asked as she raised the glass to her lips and took a sip. It tasted clean and new, like water from a mountain stream. Probably was, considering who he was.

"To them I am going to be a magically impotent Emperor and doom them to a powerless Imperial Court," he replied.

Ciardis frowned. "I don't understand."

"Where are you from?" he asked abruptly, changing the subject.

"Vaneis," she replied, swallowing hard. She was beginning to feel dizzy and nauseous, as if something were pulling at her stomach. Unsteadily she said, "Near the White Mountains. I've lived there all my life until now."

As he stayed silent in his thoughts she grabbed at her stomach and dropped the glass, gasping, "What did you poison me with?"

"Nothing," he said, startled. He saw her form begin to shimmer and said quickly, "You need to anchor yourself, or you'll go back to where you came from! The bracelet is set to your desire to stay or to come."

Just before she disappeared, Ciardis called out, "How?"

Sebastian stared at the damp circle of water on the carpet where the girl had disappeared and thought, *well, God dammit. And dreck, for that matter. She was who she said she was.*

***

Once again, Ciardis felt awash with magic. Her vision faded, and she felt as if her body were being pulled apart in a thousand different ways. It wasn't a pleasant feeling; it reminded her of a childhood incident when the blacksmith's daughter had gotten mad at Ciardis for making eyes at the farmer's boy she liked. One minute, Ciardis had been giving the boy a shy smile, and the next thing she knew, she had been in the middle of a dirty pond, coughing up water and struggling to stand up.

It was just Ciardis's rotten luck. Mary, the blacksmith's daughter, was destined to be a portal master, and Ciardis had gotten on her bad side. Mary had called it "gating." Ciardis had called it being a know-it-all bitch who used magic to get what she wanted. She had the same gut wrenching experience this time…but no Mary to explain its occurrence.

As her vision began to clear, she realized that she was in the bedroom off the memory room where her journey had begun. She promptly passed out in the large feather bed from magical fatigue.

***

She woke up to a loud clap next to her ear. There stood Serena, crowing with glee. "So it worked, then! Your powers have come in?"

Ciardis, afraid she might faint again, sat up unsteadily on the bed. She closed her eyes for a moment and then opened them again. "Yes, I guess so."

"And did you like the gift?" asked Serena.

Ciardis wondered if Serena knew what the gift really was. "It's certainly…unusual," she replied cautiously.

"Yes," said Serena, still deliriously happy. "The gemstones are quite rare. We'll make sure to get you a shorter dress to show it off on the second day of the Hunt."

"Serena?" asked Ciardis tentatively. "What is the Aether Realm?"

Serena eyed her sharply. "Where did you hear that term?"

"Around," Ciardis said vaguely. *That answers my question then. Serena had no idea the bracelet was made with residual magic - an object imbued with mage power that would be dormant until activated by the person it was intended for…*

"The Aether Realm is a dangerous, dangerous place," Serena said quietly. "It is a Middle Realm between ours and that of the Gods, and mimics our world exactly. Mages have gone there and never returned. They got so caught up in the magic of the Realm that it has been said that they could no longer feel the drain on their mage cores, which grew worse the longer they stayed."

"How do you get there?" Ciardis asked.

"You don't. *We* don't," said Serena flatly. "Only mages of great power can access that Realm. And you can only leave if they want you to. You will never go there, if I can help it," she said, twisting the rings on her fingers as she spoke. By the end of the statement, she was actually wringing her hands.

Ciardis found it weird, Serena was fidgeting. By the Gods, the woman was nervous.

"Enough of this conversation," her sponsor ordered. "Put the Aether Realm out of your mind. You need to get ready now, because one of your Patron candidates has come for a pre-interview."

"A pre-interview?" Ciardis asked. "You didn't tell me about any—"

"Don't you sass me, young woman," Serena said. "I would have had more than enough time to prepare you if you hadn't slept the day away. I have no idea what you have done, but your magical core is practically drained. It's a good thing that this pre-interview is only a formality, as opposed to a true demonstration of your weathervane abilities. You wouldn't be able to enhance a small fire with what's left of your core."

Sniffing Serena said, "That said, this Patron only wishes to meet with you in the tea parlor for a light meal. It will be a short conversation and he shows quite a keen interest in you. Let's get you changed beforehand." Ciardis nodded in acceptance and followed her out of the room and down the hall to another wing of the castle.

She was surprised when they ended up in the hammam below the castle's main hall instead of back in her room for a quick change of dress and light make-up. The hammam was a large bathing room in the basement of the castle. Ciardis liked to think of it as her own personal heaven—similar to the heated mineral pools of Vaneis, except that it was ten times more efficient and the water wasn't cloudy. The companions used it as a communal bath; it had steam rooms, massage alcoves, showers, and bathing pools. Even with a personal shower in her room, Ciardis still came down to the hammam quite often with Terris for girl chat after their Practicals. It was quite relaxing to soak in the steam and water after a long day of practice, practice, practice.

The baths served not only as a place for the women to clean themselves, but the steam heating system from the fires was also used to create steam that was piped up to heat the floors above when needed. As she and Serena entered through the main doors, Ciardis saw that three attendants awaited her: one for her hair, another to help her in the bath and to trim her body hair, and a third to powder her face and work on her nails. They were dressed in modest dresses with latched belts, and carried their tools wrapped in towels.

Bemused, she asked Serena, "Isn't my Patron waiting?"

With a wink, Serena said, "It's never too early to learn the art of keeping a man on tether. He'll wait, he'll wonder, and as long as he isn't waiting too long, he'll be salivating by the time you arrive."

Once they'd finished a nice, long half-hour later, Ciardis was escorted to the dressing room, where she slipped into a form-fitting gold dress with a sweeping skirt that matched the small golden butterfly ornaments pinned in her hair.

Before entering the parlor where her suitor waited, she turned to Serena, "Who is he?"

As the parlor doors opened, Serena whispered, "Viscount Iskas of Marce." Nodding, Ciardis stepped into the room with Lady Serena by her side.

The Viscount was rather short, she decided, shorter than she'd expected, though slim and nicely built. He was tracing his finger on a large map on display behind Venetian glass – his back to them, though surely he'd heard the door open. As he turned around, she realized with an intense shock that the Viscount was none other than Prince Sebastian from the Aether Realm.

CHAPTER TEN

If Ciardis felt shocked, it was nothing compared to the look of pleased surprise on Sebastian's face. They stared at each other for a full minute before Lady Serena stepped forward to break the silence. "My Lord Viscount, it is a pleasure and an honor to welcome you to the Companions' Guild," she said,. "We were pleased with your request for a preparatory meeting with one of our most celebrated companion trainees, Miss Ciardis Vane. We have just confirmed that she is, in fact, a Weathervane."

Ciardis felt a stab of annoyance as she stared at Sebastian. The drawing in his binder didn't look the least bit like him, and nowhere in the dossier was it mentioned that he was still a teenager, nor that "Viscount Marce" was apparently one of the Prince Heir's hereditary titles. If, indeed, it was. And what was this "Iskas" business? How many names did he have, anyway?

Cutting his eyes from Ciardis's gaze, Sebastian bowed smoothly to Lady Serena as he replied, "The pleasure is mine, Lady Serena. I hope to learn more about the woman I have become so taken with even before the Patron Hunt."

Ciardis snorted, unable to completely stop herself from laughing. The amusement she felt at the flowery language from a boy who couldn't be more than fifteen was threatening to undo her.

"Is there something wrong, Ciardis?" inquired Serena with ice in her voice as she swept forward to prepare the tea. Her icy tone promised that Ciardis had even more etiquette lessons in store for her, especially since Ciardis should have been the first to step forward and take care of pouring the tea.

"No, milady," said Ciardis quietly, horrified that Serena was serving the Prince Heir. There was no shame in that, no matter how high one's rank, but it was Ciardis's job. She felt ready to melt into the floor, but instead, she went to sit beside Sebastian on the couch, noting the weird expression on his face as she sat.

Calmly she took over Serena's task, asked Sebastian if he'd like one cube or two, and decided she was ready to throw the tea in his face after all of this secrecy. With side glances she took in his nice clothing and polite manners as best she could. As soon as Ciardis had finished serving, Lady Serena said, "I'll leave you two here until the bell tolls the half-hour. Will that do?" At his nod, she swept regally out of the parlor.

"I believe you," Sebastian said as soon as the door closed. He turned toward her, his face expressionless. "I believe that you are, in fact, who you say you are: the last Weathervane in all of Algardis. And I need your help."

Ciardis lifted a well-plucked eyebrow and raised her leg to show off the bauble encircling her left ankle above a ridiculous satin slipper. "Well, Viscount, I still don't believe you. I know next to nothing about you, but I do know this: you say you are a prince, and yet you appear on my doorstep calling yourself a viscount. Given the inaccuracies in my dossier on Viscount Marce, including who he truly is, I'm inclined to doubt the veracity of either claim."

"I'm not Iskas," admitted Sebastian. "That much is true. I had my guardsman forge his personal papers in order to be considered for your patronage. But I lied about that for a very good reason." He took a deep breath and stood, adjusting his tunic. Another green one to match his eyes, she noticed. "I couldn't very well apply as myself. Anyone tied to me is in peril, as you saw yesterday in the Aether Realm. My real name is Sebastian Athanos Algardis." He said the words in a rush, as if he knew that if he didn't get it out now, he wouldn't have the courage to keep going.

Ciardis looked him over doubtfully before she burst out laughing, hands clutching her stomach. "I've heard some hogwash," she said, "but your tale, milord, takes the cake." She stood up and rested her hands on her hips. "Do you really expect me to believe that I stand before the heir to the throne, who is posing as a Viscount, *and* that he wants my help?"

Sebastian pinched the bridge of his nose as if to ward off a coming headache. "Yes, I do."

"Ha!" she said, throwing up her hands. She paced the room. "It figures. The nobles all want to mock the poor, powerless, and country companion." Angrily, she turned around in a swirl of golden fabric. "Do you really think I'm not worthy of a patron's choice?"

"I assure you, I'm not here to mock you," Sebastian said, lifting his hands in a placating gesture. "You're quite worthy, believe me." He looked a bit flustered. "And...and you're quite...well, beaut...*valuable*. In fact, the power you loaned me in the Aether is probably only a fraction of your abilities. You saved my life today."

Ciardis wasn't yet ready to give in and believe him, but she had been there in the Aether with him, had stood against his foes, and knew that they, at least, believed he was the Prince Heir. She came back to the couch he stood next to, plopped down, and grabbed a biscuit from the tea service. "Let's say I decide to believe you, Sebastian Athanos Algardis," she said, pronouncing each syllable carefully. "How could I possibly help the Prince Heir? What can I do that your fabled Gardis cannot?"

He sat down beside her as he answered her question with one of his own. "Do you know the history of the Empire's formation? Did they teach you of the tie between the first emperor and the land?"

Stiffly, she replied, "I've heard of the breaking, yes. The first emperor came from Sahalia, across the seas. He was a powerful protector of his people and loved his land. As emperor he made a pact. Out of this pact rose the Guardians, known as Al-Gardis, and a binding contract to keep the land of Algardis whole and thriving through blood and sweat for as long as his family ruled."

Sebastian nodded, impressed at her knowledge. "Yes," he said. "Most are familiar with the Gardis because they are the pact personified—direct descendants of the unions between the first five Emperors and their ladies in the Imperial Halls. They train their entire lives, from birth to death, to protect the land from evil and the people from tyranny."

"But there's another side to the pact, one drawn in blood," he continued. "In the first decade of the Empire's founding, the emperor faced challenges from all sides. The enemy in the North wanted to wipe out Algardis. The emperor's dragonkin of Sahalia saw him and his subjects as human chattel to be broken and enslaved, and the kith—natives of the lands that became the Empire—fought back at every turn, as they were displaced by homesteaders. With his army of just a few thousand soldiers, the first emperor knew that he could not hold back the invaders on all fronts."

"So he made a pact with the spirit of the land, the Land Wight, an elemental of immense power. The Land Wight agreed to create a powerful physical barrier around Algardis for the first one hundred years of its existence, and to protect it from invasions from land, sea, and air. In return, the first emperor agreed to tie his line to the land for its future protection."

Ciardis wasn't quite convinced. "So you're saying that every single emperor since the first emperor Athanos has been tied to the land?"

"Every emperor and Imperial child," Sebastian clarified.

"And what does that tie mean for the Imperial children?" she questioned.

"Each child," he said, "is tied to a portion of Algardis that they are connected to from birth. As long as that child is alive and the bond is strong, the land will thrive, crops will flourish, and disease will be abated."

Ciardis knew plague still pulsed through the land in waves, and people still died, so how could these Imperial children be so powerful if the land lay fallow? Dozens of young ones back home had died last winter, the coldest Vaneis had seen in decades, and she had heard of worse in the far northern reaches of the Empire.

"As Prince Heir and the firstborn child of my father," Sebastian said, tiredly wiping his eyes, "I should be able to protect the whole of Algardis. By birth and by blood, the entire Empire is and forever will be under my protection. Historically, the more powerful the heir, the better off the land will be, and, by extension, the more powerful the Imperial court will be."

"What does the nobility have to do with this?" she asked.

He sighed and explained, "Over time, the Imperial line has married into multiple noble families, so they, too, enjoy some of the heritage of the blood ties. In essence, every person with Imperial blood has become a mortal Land Wight, to one extent or another," he said. "But that heritage and their access to it is tied into the power of the Emperor."

"I see. But by your logic, they wouldn't hate the Prince Heir. They need you. You're their link to power and privilege." Tilting her head Ciardis said, "Unless you messed that up somehow. What'd you do?"

He gave her a wry grin. "You catch on quickly. My father is getting older, and it's assumed that I will ascend to the throne within ten years. But I haven't been able to manifest a connection to the land since I was about five. I have no idea why. Essentially, they believe that I'm blocking their power."

Ciardis wracked her brain for the history of the last five Emperors as she took a demure sip of tea. "The nobility are right to be worried, I think," she said. "May the Heavens protect the Emperor. Sadly the past five rulers have rarely lived past fifty years. There's only one that I can remember, and he died at sixty-two."

Sebastian nodded. "My grandfather, Cymus. The connection to the land takes a toll on all those who bear it. The nobles are afraid— not without cause, as you say—that I'll ascend to the throne and, as a consequence, they will lose their power, their connection to their own domains, and will be unable to use those ties to the land to stop the Northern hordes from pouring across the border."

"They don't seem too far off the mark."

"Tell me something I don't know." Sebastian grimaced. "I understand their fears, and I'm afraid, too. But I also know something they don't." Ciardis looked at him silently, inviting him to continue. "Despite what they think, I'm not completely ignorant of the land; I can feel every vibration, every forest, every mountain, every vale, and every swamp. It's only my ability to manipulate that connection that has dwindled."

He slumped forward with a hangdog look in his eyes. "I can sense the land, but my ability is out of focus." Looking at her with a pleading expression—though Ciardis wasn't sure if he was pleading with her, or some invisible god to answer his prayers—he continued, "The land is there for me, but it's too powerful for me to grab by myself. If I were still a child, the Land Wight would help me as I slowly regained my heritage, piece by piece."

Ciardis shook her head, "Why didn't it?"

"Why didn't it what?" said Sebastian in confusion.

"You've been powerless for over a decade. Couldn't it have stepped in before?"

Frustration crossed Sebastian's face, "I don't know why. But now, as a man, I must do it without its help."

Ciardis felt like muttering some choice words about a boy who had yet to shave calling himself a man, but held back. Some clans marked the thirteenth year as the beginning of manhood, and apparently Clan Algardis was one of them. Ciardis looked Sebastian in the eyes and said, "Fine. Let's say I believe everything—the Land Wight, the heritage, the threat. Why didn't Lady Serena recognize you for who you really are? She's been to court plenty of times. You wear no glamour."

Sebastian shifted uncomfortably as he wrung his hands, much as Serena herself had done earlier. "Actually, I do. It's not one which affects the actual physical perception, but rather the mind's understanding of that visual."

Pulling back a sleeve, he exposed his wrist. A thin bracelet encircled it, similar in make to Ciardis's moonstone and sapphire anklet. The gemstones were a bit different, but just barely. In fact, it was so similar that Ciardis reached down to pull up her skirt to compare the ornament on her ankle to the one he wore. "I used it to interrupt the connection between what Serena's eyes saw and what her mind perceived," Sebastian said. "Rather than change my physical appearance, the Mindas bracelet that I wear on my wrist replaced it."

"I see. So if you're the mystery patron who gave me this bracelet, why didn't you believe me in the Aether Realm?" she said with an angry gesture at the twin piece of jewelry that encircled her ankle.

"Wouldn't you have doubts about some woman who'd shown up in a forest with no way to verify her claims? Even one who was wearing the correct bracelet? I had no idea what you looked like."

Ciardis nearly rolled her eyes as she thought, *Great minds think alike, eh?*

"Now that I know you are indeed the Weathervane who has all of high society rubbing their hands with glee we can move forward."

"Move forward?" Ciardis murmured smoothly, taking another sip of tea. "And what, pray tell, would we move forward with?"

"As a prospective patron, I intend to court you and win the contract," he said with the full arrogance of youth.

"And if I have no intention of being shackled to a fifteen-year-old boy?" she shot back.

"I'll be sixteen in a month," he said. Sebastian seemed honestly taken aback by her implied refusal. Most companions would consider it a credit to the Companions' Guild to be so hotly pursued, or at the very least suitably impressed to be courted by one of noble—let alone Imperial—blood. "I assure you," he said curtly, "I can make it worth your while."

"No, you can't," said Ciardis flatly. "I may be inexperienced, but I'm not stupid. Your own courtiers are trying to kill you, and your social standing is next to nil. Any of my other prospective Patrons would be a much more suitable pick, in particular because they want me for me. You need me, but for how long?"

Sebastian opened and closed his mouth. He bit his lip, thinking, apparently trying to come up with something that would convince her to accept his proposal. Then, hesitantly, he said, "You're right— I'm not offering you a marriage, a family, or a warm hearth to crochet by. I'm offering you an adventure, and a chance to save your Empire. Everyone needs something to inspire them, and can you really say that managing household accounts will do that for you?"

Ciardis swallowed hard and looked away. His little speech had hit close to home; that was exactly what she had to look forward to if she accepted Barnaren's proposal, and no doubt many of the other proposals. Household accounts, birthing baby after baby, and decorating. Homemaker and broodmare. Her face twitched slightly as she thought with guilt, *Is this any different from what would have awaited me as the wife of Fervis Miller?*

Snapping out of her reverie, Ciardis grabbed Sebastian's wrist, and turned the Mindas bracelet back and forth to look at it, "So you have enough wealth to buy a fancy trinket. What makes you think this will save you?"

Sebastian said stiffly, "These aren't trinkets. They're Imperial Armory treasures imbued with Residual Magic. You can't just saunter down to the Fifth Street market and ask for five at a time. With all the spells woven into them, it takes dozens of mages to create either one. It did, in fact."

"I'm tired of this game," he announced. Reaching over his shoulders to grab the button flap tying his jacket at his neck he took the cloth from his left shoulder, under his right arm and over his left shoulder revealing bare skin. He turned his back and bared his right shoulder to her. "If I can't convince you to help me out of loyalty to king and country, perhaps you'll take legitimacy."

On his shoulder, Sebastian bore the sigil of the Imperial Courts: a lion rampant before a stone wall. But this sigil was more than it seemed, for in the lion's mouth was a giant ruby. As he turned back to her, she almost squirmed. Sebastian said, "Before my mother died, she had my father sign an agreement in blood that stated that I could choose and marry whomever I desired. The blood-red marriage stone symbolizes that. If you really want marriage, I can give that to you."

Ciardis was touched, but her voice was wary as she said, "As sweet as that sounds, we're going to have to think of something else. Given your age, some would say that I…influenced you unduly as an older woman. Nevertheless, I swear to you, Prince Sebastian Athanos Algardis, that I will help you in your quest to vanquish your enemies."

He refastened his waist jacket, looking pleased, as Ciardis said, "If I'm to help you, Your Highness, I'll need to know exactly what you desire of me. Surely a beautiful woman on your arm is not enough to ward off assassins."

"As you remember from our time in the Aether Realm, it certainly isn't. What I need from you is not your beauty or grace, but your talent. As the only Weathervane born in nearly four decades, you are my only hope to harness the Land Wight's gift and restore my power."

"My talent is to raise another person's power, Your Grace. You have none."

"'Your Grace' is what you call a duke," he corrected her. "At the very least, you must call me 'Your Highness,' or better yet, 'Your Imperial Majesty.'"

Her eyes flashed, and he quickly said, "Joking—just joking. Okay? And as much as it pains me to say so, you're wrong about my power. I didn't say I had none, I said I can't *access* it. I know it's there, and bountiful. If anything, the jump to my palace apartment from the Aether Realm proved that. You enhanced what I thought had been permanently locked away. Otherwise, we would have never gotten out of the Aether Realm alive. After all, the bracelet you wear is keyed only to you, not to myself. And before you ask, no, Weathervanes cannot enhance the power that already resides in residual magical objects – whatever level of power it has been imbued with is the one it will stay with."

She got up and began to pace again. "So what exactly are you offering? Will you contest for my Patronage as the Prince Heir of the

Algardis Empire? Or is this just a one-time boost for Iskas?"

He rubbed his head tiredly. "Gods, I don't know. I need to search the Imperial libraries again. I don't think you'll be able to enhance my powers permanently without a constant link, but I'm not sure. Do you know if a link is needed?"

"I will have to ask around," she said.

At that moment, the clock tolled the half-hour, and Lady Serena came back into the room, true to her word. Beaming, she said, "I do hope you two had a productive conversation."

Ciardis nodded primly. Sebastian bowed and said, "Yes, very. I'm eager to see Ms. Weathervane again during the Hunt."

"Very well, Viscount Marce," said Lady Serena. "Shall I escort you out?"

He nodded in agreement and took Ciardis's hand, kissing it lightly. She couldn't help but wrinkle her nose as he left. Prince Heir or not, Sebastian's hand-kissing technique, with a bit too much saliva involved, left a lot to be desired.

CHAPTER ELEVEN

The next morning Ciardis decided to take advantage of the seasonal opening of the Imperial gardens. Once every four months the Emperor decreed the court gardens were open to all who desired entrance. Ciardis scribbled a note to Serena and Damias to inform them of where she'd gone and that she'd be back in time for this afternoon's lessons in the gardens.

Taking the *tuk-tuk* she came to the garden's gate. Seeing the sign that asked for a bit of coin to offset the cost of repairs after public displays, she gave the garden assistant a few shillings as she passed through the entrance. Deciding she wanted the freedom to wander alone with her thoughts she avoided the group of newcomers heading for a servant who would guide them around.

Soon she was walking on a path that was empty except for the rustle of winds and the beautiful plants that adorned it. An hour into her wandering, she noticed that she was in an older part of the gardens with huge sycamore trees that had roots that arced from the ground. Ducking under a root the height of a human, she found an old palace gate leading to a door on the other side - rusted over but unlocked.

Deciding to take a peak Ciardis walked through the hallways occasionally touching a marble bust with cobwebs caked over it and fabric draped from the windows which had long ago begun rotting.

I must be in the old Imperial Palace.

Just before she turned a corner she heard voices up ahead. Deciding now was not the time to make her unsanctioned presence known she ducked back around the corner and into an unused nook behind a very large suit of dragon armor.

The voices came closer.

"Milady, the time is almost near," said a man. "Soon the boy will be fully discredited. You will take your rightful place."

"With you by my side – I assume Marcus," said a woman's calculating voice.

"I live only to serve, milady," he said.

"Yes, do remember who you *truly* serve here. It is not my fool brother and certainly not that brat of a nephew."

As they passed her Ciardis only saw their backs. They reached the far end of the corridor from where Ciardis hid and parted ways.

Ciardis waited quietly for a long time before she emerged from her spot behind the armor. Rushing back she ran out of the gate and under the sycamore's roots. Her dress was ruined with the trailing cobwebs and dust but she didn't even consider that.

As she slowed her fast pace down upon reaching the normal gardens she tried to recall exactly what she had heard. She really wasn't sure. Who was that woman? A feeling of fear crept up Ciardis's spine until she almost screamed aloud when she felt a hand grip her wrist.

She did startle and whirl around though.

"Easy lass," said a man who stood in front of her. "I mean you no harm."

He held his hands out to show how harmless he was. It didn't help – he was a man with towering stature. But her training kicked in.

"Of course milord," Ciardis said. "It is I who should be apologizing. I was merely startled."

He gave her a grin and bow, "Lord Aaron, at your service my dear."

Ciardis couldn't have been more mortified. Here she stood with cobwebs on her dress and dirt in her hair – before quite a handsome man. *Once just ONCE why can't I be like Patricia? Perfectly presentable every minute of every day.*

Gathering her pride and displaying a sunny smile took a lot of courage but Ciardis managed it. "It's a pleasure to make your acquaintance milord. I am Ciardis Weathervane and I do believe you've caught me on a bad day."

"Well," he said, "I do believe I have." He eyed her while rubbing his chin.

"Since we're here together," he said "Shall we make a wager?"

"A wager milord?" she asked.

"Perhaps it would be better to call it a proposal, Lady Weathervane," he said with a mischievous look.

Ciardis stiffened. How did he know?

"If you can boost my power enough for me to lift both of our bodies in the air," he continued, "I will make sure not to inform your mentors of your…disheveled appearance."

"And how would you know my mentors?"

"There's only one Weathervane in all the land my dear. And the golden eyes you bear are your key."

Ciardis didn't see any way out of this. If she agreed to the bargain her skulking around the palace would be kept secret. If she didn't it would be one more thing Serena could hold against her.

"Then I think I can handle that milord."

"Well then," he said as he reached for her hand, "let's see what you can do."

Dipping in to her mage core Ciardis noted with surprise how powerful Aaron's power looked to be. Why he needed her help in this was mystery to her but who was she to doubt his intentions?

Upon tapping into the core she released her power and boosted his in the process. Feeling her efforts he called to the wind to pick them up. They rose softly in the air one foot, two feet, and three feet on a thick cloud of compressed air. When they stopped and levitated where they were Ciardis smiled in wonder. She could see the garden for miles. It helped that she was also holding the hands of a handsome man.

He set them down minutes later and walked off whistling without another word between them.

***

Later that day Ciardis sat in the Guild gardens unsure of whether or not she should bring up the earlier incident in the Imperial gardens with Serena. Even though she and Lord Aaron had made some sort of pact in general, it was better to be safe than sorry. Hidden things tended to not stay hidden. Not for very long anyway.

Presently, she sat with the other trainees, swathed in her full Hunt regalia. They had put up sun canopies of silk cloth and seated each of the trainees in portable boudoirs. With her lips painted, powder ghosting across her face, and a stiff corset laced to her waist, Ciardis felt like another person, perhaps even a fraud. But she sat still and fought not to fidget. The damn corset *hurt*.

She watched carefully as the companion recruits paraded down the aisle. They were there to display composure in adverse conditions – in this case stifling heat and dripping makeup. She felt sympathy for them, as the sun was shining harshly down on them as they struggled to maintain composure under thick layers of satin and silk. Ciardis had tried to refuse the thick silk dress and the heavy corset, but Damias had made her wear both, and carry a parasol to boot. *Its good practice for your Hunt*, Ciardis mimicked.

As she sat thinking, Lady Serena appeared by her side. She looked sharply at the other girls, and they quickly moved away from the duo, leaving Ciardis and Serena alone to talk. "It has been a full week since you gained your powers, Ciardis," Serena said.

Ciardis nodded hesitantly, not quite sure where this conversation was going. She had felt like bringing the garden encounter up but Serena's angry disposition quickly put those thoughts far from her mind.

"Seven days, fourteen hours, and two minutes, to be exact," said Serena. "And yet, there's not been one sign of what you can do."

Ciardis hadn't had a chance to do anything, and said as much. "With respect, Lady Serena, how am I supposed to demonstrate my powers? I've not had a chance to use them."

"Precisely," said Serena. "Which is why I've arranged for you to begin your Hunt in a different fashion than the other candidates."

Ciardis turned to her, her curiosity piqued. "What do you mean?"

Serena reveled in the secret she held for a moment. *Oh, how she loves doing that*, Ciardis fumed silently. When Serena saw Ciardis begin to fidget in impatience, she sighed. "As you know, Ciardis, the first day of the Patron Hunt for each prospective companion is supposed to be unique. Everyone can decide to hold their own event but the usual practice is to choose to hold a Salon of the Arts to impress their patrons with their knowledge of music and culture. Which is why standing out from the pack by being unique is a much better idea. You, my dear, will be the talk of society for days to come! You have elected to hold a formal Blood Hunt!"

"Have I?" asked Ciardis, a bit dazed. "A true Blood Hunt?"

"Yes," said Serena. "General Barnaren has graciously agreed to sponsor a hunt of the white hart elk outside the city, and as such, he will be your primary focus. You will need to impress upon him your skills in riding, archery, and tracking. But most importantly, you must give him the mage strength to hold and slay the white hart elk."

"Well," said Ciardis – exasperated that she hadn't been consulted, "I don't know what to say, Serena."

"Oh, I just knew you'd be ecstatic about this!" Serena said. "You can thank me when you've landed a Patron to rival all others."

"Of course," Ciardis murmured. "And where are we to find these elk? If I'm not mistaken, we're in Sandrin Bay, land of beaches, hot sun, and cool winds—hardly a deep forest with crags and valleys for these elusive creatures to live within."

"Oh, dear, of course we won't be hunting anywhere near the Sandrin city limits," Serena said, her sugary tone just barely hiding the sharpness of her words. She'd never been a fan of Ciardis's dry sarcasm, particularly because Serena was never quite sure when it was directed at her. "We'll be taking the Genur portal way to Askavi Vale, near the Nardes border."

"I'll have the servants pack your things for a daytrip. You must bring riding dresses, as well as tunics," Serena said. "You will need to impress upon the general your tenacity and flexibility—in other words, you must ride as fast as he, ride as hard as he, and you must never let anyone else get a clean shot at that elk."

"Oh and Ciardis?" Serena said. "Before you go on the hunt – I have a small task for you. You're to bring a bottle of rare perfume to the Princess Heir's chambers…as a gift."

"Of course, Serena."

Ciardis sat back and turned her attention back to duties as the remaining group of trainees arranged themselves in front of the garden podium, pretending that the hot sun and humidity weren't bothering them in the slightest. Ciardis sighed. She was up next – this time it was sidesaddle performances.

An hour later she headed off in a gilded carriage to the palace gates. Explaining her tasks to the servants was not easy but it helped to look haughty and sweep forward like she owned the entire Empire. After speaking with two butlers and a chambermaid she was directed to the quarters of the Princess Heir.

As she stood outside waiting to be received, Ciardis anxiously watched the sunset. She was ready to go home.

A servant dressed in high-quality clothes stepped out into the audience chamber. "The Princess Heir is indisposed but I will accept the gift in her stead," he explained.

"Very well," said Ciardis while handing over the perfume package with the signed note from Lady Serena. As she walked away she heard a voice drift out from the cracked door of the Princess Heir's sitting room.

Oddly enough it sounded like the woman from before.

***

The following morning, Ciardis awoke before the sun rose. She dressed and went down to the stables to oversee the packing of her mules and to pick a sturdy but fast steed for her Hunt. As she bridled and saddled her chosen horse, a bright chestnut filly with a fast trot and a good jumping record, she couldn't help but look forward to seeing the outside of the city.

Many of her fellow trainees would have turned up their noses at this opportunity, but for Ciardis, it was a chance to be different, a chance to show that growing up with capable hands wasn't so bad. At least, she hoped the general would see it that way.

As she and Damias moved out, the first rays of the sun gilded the city gates. Damias rode beside her on a roan gelding. His hat sat jauntily on his head, and he held the reins with the confidence of a man born in the saddle. Ciardis gave him a surprised look as he rode up next to her. "Not many nobles bother to learn how to ride a non-winged horse," she commented.

"True, but my mother was a wanderer. As a child, I learned that not every Empire has pegasi so that we can fly in the heavens or plush carriages to travel within. Sometimes we even rode on mule-back. Once, in the mountains of the North, I was even carried across the pass between the White Mountains by a Yeti."

Ciardis stared at him, shocked. "And your mother let you ride that beast – a Yeti? Their claws alone are the size of a small child!"

"Not only did my mother let that white-haired beast carry me, she insisted on it." Damias responded dryly, "We were going up some steep cliffs and she said that its wide feet and sharp claws were the only thing that would allow us to get up the icy paths at anything approaching a normal speed."

Ciardis chuckled. "Your mother sounds like a hard woman."

"Yes, she was—and still is," Damias said proudly.

They reached the Genur portal way around midmorning. Glancing at his traveling companion, Damias asked, "Have you ever been through a portal way?"

"No," Ciardis responded softly, gazing at it in wonder. It was a very large, gray metal ring. To her, it looked wide enough to accommodate three men standing abreast, or one very small carriage. The circle stood on a raised platform with stone steps approaching the front. Off to either side of the portal two wide ramps arcing up from the west and east made up the wings. The metal ring was embedded in the stone platform below it so that the ring stood freestanding, proud and high above the sparse grass and the trees that encircled it.

Two gatekeepers stood beside the massive gate, one on either side. Ciardis squinted, but couldn't make out the insignia on their jackets. Damias walked over to one of the men—to give him instructions, she supposed. After a few short words, he walked back, gave her a wide grin, and said, "Get ready."

Ciardis managed a weak smile and clutched her cloak closer around her. The gateman turned to a small console; she realized that his body had been blocking it from her sight. Ciardis half turned to Damias to ask about the console, careful to keep an eye on the portal way itself.

Pointing it out, "What's that small blocky thing?"

"That's the gate keypad," he explained. "Any person can work it, as long as they have proper access to the keystone."

Interesting. Ciardis strained her eyes to catch the gateman's actions, but she was standing a little too far away. Damias noticed her intent stare and explained, "It's a standing portalway. One of the few ways to jump across the empire as a larger group. Of course, most people prefer to travel in smaller pairs or individually. It's less unsettling."

"Unsettling?" she asked. "That doesn't sound very nice."

"It's not," he said. "Your stomach will be in turmoil for the first five minutes after you've gone through."

Looking back at the portal way, she saw that it had flattened into a pool of rippling light. The head guard called out, "Riders up!"

They went through in pairs. As they passed through the gate, the faint buzzing sensation exacerbated until she was hunched over her mare's neck and tears were flowing down her cheeks.

They emerged on the other side to find a panoply of tents, horses in paddocks, and a group of people awaiting them on the hilltop.

"Turmoil?" she gasped out as she sat up on her horse. "That was like being punched in the stomach. *Twice.*" Damias looked over at her with a weak grin, "It can be for the first time…and for the twentieth. Would you have gone through so easily if I had told you that?"

She scowled at him.

Out of the group strode a gentleman of early middle age with a strong face. He wore a leather jerkin over a tunic and breeches. The only ornaments to indicate his exalted status were the deep red general's cloak that flared at his shoulders and the gold ring set with a red on his right hand. Pausing directly in front of Ciardis, he smiled and reached up to take her tanned hand in the firm grip of his light brown one.

She wasn't surprised at his forwardness. A man like Barnaren wouldn't be shy or indirect. She had studied Barnaren's history and knew he'd led just as many battles from the front lines as he had from the strategy tent. His courtship of her wouldn't be any less direct. The numerous scars on his face and the calluses she felt on his hand bespoke of a lifetime of battles and skirmishes fought on behalf of the Emperor.

Smiling shyly, she dismounted the filly and bowed with a slight bend of her knees. She'd been taught never to attempt a curtsy in pants; she'd just end up looking ridiculous. "General Barnaren," she said. "It is a pleasure to make your acquaintance."

He gave her a smile and bowed in return. "It is I, my dear, who is most pleased to meet such a beautiful and capable young woman. I have heard tales, but your beauty exceeds them all."

Beside Barnaren stood a younger man who could have been his twin if he hadn't been at least fifteen years younger. The man smiled at the general's praise of Ciardis, but his smile didn't quite reach his steel-gray eyes. She could see the disdain from his posture; if he could have wrinkled his nose in distaste, something not allowed in polite company, he would have.

The general turned, "This is Corporal SaBarnaren."

Ciardis was surprised. The man was General Barnaren's son – his bastard son. In the Empire all children born out of wedlock were given one of two names upon birth – Algardian, if they weren't being cared for by their parents and were a ward of the state, or the prefix of 'Sa' next to their birth parent's name. Corporal SaBarnaren was one of those children borne from an unmarried union.

As he introduced his bastard son, Ciardis's face betrayed no emotion. She offered her hand in greeting. "A pleasure to meet you, Corporal SaBarnaren," Ciardis said with mischief in her brown eyes as she met SaBarnaren's gaze. She would not hold his heritage against him. Being a darker skinned daughter of a wayfarer in the vale had given her as much or more grief as a person born a bastard.

Raising a smooth eyebrow, he responded with a mocking half-smile, "The pleasure is mine, Mistress Weathervane."

As she shook his hand, she felt the electric shock of his power on her skin. Ah, things had just gotten interesting. Bastards were fine; mage bastards were another thing entirely. He hadn't presented a threat before, but now that she knew of his power it would be dangerous to ignore. She needed to talk to Serena as soon as possible.

Stepping away from the two gentlemen, she turned to contemplate the riding party they had brought with them while gathering her thoughts. The laws of the land were clear – Corporal SaBarnaren stood to inherit the Barnaren lands via magical inheritance rights as long as a child of legal birthright and magical ability didn't supersede his claim. If she accepted General Barnaren's proposal and agreed to have his child, SaBarnaren could pose a threat to that child's life, as it would be the only person that stood between him and inheritance. People had started wars for less.

Family had killed for less.

In deep thought Ciardis gathered her cloak around her, and the general called out in a loud baritone, "All riders mount! The hunt begins!"

After saddling up, they advanced to the crest of the hill, and Ciardis took in the lands that spread out in front of the hunting party. After a small dip in the hillside, a flat grassland spread out west and east, as far as the eye could see. Perhaps a hundred yards ahead, a dark forest brooded. As the filly snorted and danced a little to the side, eager to begin the race, Ciardis reined her back and whispered, "Soon, my pet, soon."

She turned her gaze on the forest ahead. It was a deep, dark wood, a suitable habitat for the fabled white hart elk they hunted today. The white fur of the elk was prized for its beauty and the softness, as well as its ability to repel water and snow. The elk only came this far south into the warm lands during breeding season—a three-week period when the elk wandered the forest in plentiful numbers.

Beside her Damias whispered, "There will be many elk throughout this forest but we want an elk with a rack that spans the sky for the General. Remember that."

Underneath her, the filly shifted impatiently, waiting for the signal to move. Ciardis checked the heft of her glaive. She was a bit nervous; just because the elks tended to be solitary didn't mean this would be an easy hunt. Hunting those huge herbivores was never easy. Male and female alike bore huge antlers on their heads for defense and rutting challenges, and of course their fur repelled not only the weather, but also most mundane weapons, including arrows and hunting spears not laced with the sedative verbane. Moreover, they were able to blend into the forest with great skill; it would be especially easy for them to hide in a forest alive with green magic.

They could be wounded with lesser weapons, but the only way to kill a white hart elk was to direct a magical attack to the heart or slash its throat with a sword. Ciardis momentarily closed her eyes as she imagined wielding the blade that would kill one of the mighty elk. In her vision, the great beast's blood spilled onto the dark forest loam, the bright red standing out against the animal's white fur, as it bellowed its last breath.

She would have no choice but to kill it; the general would expect no less.

It wasn't that she was squeamish; she'd killed and skinned her own dinner many a time back in Vaneis. But that didn't mean she enjoyed killing for sport.

Damias was on her right. He reached for her hand and gripped it as he quietly said, "Enjoy the hunt, my dear, but not the kill. And above all, smile for your Patron. If he enjoys this, then so will you."

A strange blend of eagerness, anticipation, and wariness stirred within Ciardis, and she replied, "Of course."

CHAPTER TWELVE

The horns of the honor guard sounded somewhere off to the east, and they were off in a whirlwind of hoof beats. Ciardis's filly soon took the lead, outpacing Damias's gelding and nearing the big black stallion that the general rode. With a glance at the stallion the general rode, Ciardis noted that it was a fire steed with flames snorting from his nose, embers forming his eyes, and a mane which was a flickering vision of black fire.

She wasn't afraid—not of the fire steed, nor his master. As she flicked her gaze up at the general, meeting his assessing steely eyes, Ciardis gave him a mocking salute and urged her filly ahead. For his part, Barnaren seemed pleasantly surprised at the fire he saw in the young girl's eyes.

As their party thundered into the woods, a clear path appeared in front of them between a long line of oaks and tall maples. The general urged the fire steed ahead of Ciardis and the pack and then he abruptly whirled around to face the group. They came thundering to stop in a semi-circle before him.

"Mason, come forward and have your dogs lead us to the nearest beast's lair," he called. A young man with auburn hair urged his horse forward. Jostling around his steed were six nose hounds, all clearly straining for the scent and eager to be loosed. Jumping down from his horse into the middle of the pack, Mason took a white patch of fur out of one coat pocket and passed it under the nose of each of his hounds, careful to make sure they all got a whiff. At his signal, they put their noses to the ground, searching for a trail. When it became clear that they wanted to continue north, he mounted his horse and gave the general his news.

"Very well," the general replied, satisfied. "Let us ride, then."

They hunted the scent of the elk through the thick woods and down to the riverside, across a ford, and back through into denser foliage. The woods became so dense with low-hanging branches and underbrush that the riders had to dismount after a time in order to continue. Soon enough dirt coated her boots and branches caught in her hair. Ciardis decided to walk her mare off to the right where the path looked a little clearer, not far from the general's side, but behind him.

She was worried. They'd been hunting for two hours so far with not an elk to be seen. And she couldn't stay out here forever. She needed to impress Barnaren with enough time left to return home to prepare for the first ball that evening. *I'm lucky that none of my other prospective patrons elected to join us on this Hunt*, she thought with amusement. *It's difficult enough impressing one with briars in my hair and mud on my boots.*

A piercing whisper came from the northwest. Ciardis looked up to see the hunts master raising and lowering his right arm to signal the hunting party to go to ground. Sighing in irritation she lay down, trying to wipe her face on the only clean spot left on her tunic and then pick a briar out of her curls.

A voice interrupted her thoughts with a droll observation. "If you want to impress my father, it's best to forget about pretty dresses and jewelry and face paint. He wants a woman who can start a campfire, prepare a warrior's armor, and nock an arrow with the speed of a trained bowman."

Ciardis rose from where she was crouched at the base of a tall tree. She'd been there since the hunt master had given the all-quiet signal—an order for everyone to melt into the forest as best they could. Even the horses stood silent. She turned to Corporal SaBarnaren with an insincere smile on her lips and said, "Well, milord, it sounds as if your father seeks a squire, when I heard that what he actually needs is a wife."

"Address me as Evan, please," Corporal SaBarnaren said. "And what do you know about being a wife?"

"A bit more than you would," she murmured. The horn sounded once more, signaling the parties to move forward.

SaBarnaren dipped his head in acknowledgement, looking genuinely amused as the group began moving north.

Ciardis decided she would rather not run into him again, and elected to maneuver a bit to the northeast, circling around to catch up with the hunting party that rode west. Shading her eyes as she looked up, she saw a jagged piece of rock rising above the trees ahead of her. She thought, *Perhaps I can catch a glimpse of one of those fabled elk from that bluff.*

The filly wouldn't make it up the steep slope, though, so she left her reins looped to a branch. Ciardis climbed the ridge carefully, trying to grab handholds in the rock and clutching the edge of the rim tightly until she could hoist herself onto the ridge. After dusting herself off, she paused to catch her breath, grimacing at a pain in her leg where she'd banged it on the cliff.

As she crept to the front of the upward-sloping ledge, she made sure to maintain her footing. No sense in making it all the way to the top only to take an undignified tumble. As she reached the far ledge, she lay flat on her belly and eased forward to the edge.

As she poked her head over the cliffside, her loose chestnut curls cascaded over her eyes, and she pushed the curls back behind her ears in irritation. She saw that her earlier suspicions were correct – she could get a good view here. Looking down she was right above a small glade scattered with beautiful trees and a dark pool of water. Small, winged creatures flitted around in the pillars of sunlight that pierced the canopy of leaves above. It looked too perfect to be real, so Ciardis decided to investigate this further.

She slipped over the crest of the hill and ventured down into the shade of the trees. As she reached the far edge of her cover, she saw it—or, rather, him. A white hart elk stag stood alone in the shade near the pool.

The animal was far grander than anything that had previously been described to her. He stood a magnificent sixteen hands high, with white fur that shone like moonlight on still water. If they had stood face-to-face, his muzzle would have come to the top of her forehead; his rack of tines, with at least a dozen points spread toward the sky, reached two feet higher.

As he came forward into the sunlight of the grove, his hooves lightly disturbed the ground so that faint clouds of dust and pollen rose up around his feet. She couldn't help but think how beautiful he was. At the lake's edge, he paused and looked right at her, his breath misting in the afternoon sun, eyes like a starless midnight.

Ciardis had nothing but a bow and quiver of arrows on her, both of which were strapped to her back at the moment. If she unlimbered the bow and nocked the arrow too slowly, he might charge her, or run far enough into the forest that he'd be out of range. Her glaive— the only handheld weapon she was capable of handling, according to

Damias—was back with her filly. And even if it were here, she wasn't certain she could throw it with enough force. Or even if she should; glaives weren't designed like spears and it was more likely to fall into the deep loam on the glade floor.

Quietly, she rose out of her hiding place and stepped forward, afraid of startling the elk. But he stood calm and majestic before her, occasionally pawing the ground. She was filled with wonder as she continued to approach him – wary that he would spook at any moment. He lowered his head to nuzzle her face with a wet nose, and Ciardis laughed in delight. Raising her hand hesitantly, she stroked the soft white fur on his cheek. When he didn't flinch away, she trailed her hand up his neck and then down to his shoulder.

She knew that she should send some sort of signal to the other hunters—Evan, at least, seemed able to hear her thoughts—but she just couldn't.

"You're gorgeous," she whispered. "A true king of the forest. Why are you here? You must know that hunters stalk these woods. Run away!"

The great white elk snorted.

As she rested her hand on his cheek, she felt a magical disturbance, as if someone else were brushing at her mind. Hesitantly, she lowered the mental barriers to her mind. She'd worked hard with Damias to be able to feel when a telepath was reading her thoughts and how to block their intrusions. Dropping those mental barriers and letting someone in intentionally left her concerned and wary. The general's commanding voice flowed into her mind: *I'm coming up on your left. No, do not look. Stay still. Stay silent.*

Ciardis's breath caught, but she had no time to wonder at his telepathic abilities. She looked up into the beast's eyes, heartsick over what was about to happen. The white hart elk saw the apology in her eyes, and understood. He backed away and reared up on his hind legs. An arrow came out of the sky from Barnaren's direction and pierced the elk's chest. Ciardis stumbled back, falling to the ground before the rearing elk.

She stared at the longbow arrow jutting from the animal's ribs. However, it wasn't enough to bring him down. Only a blade or magical blast to the heart could do that. In pain and fury, the white hart elk whirled around to face his tormentor. He saw the general a dozen feet away and charged. Ciardis watched as the elk raced toward the general, who now clutched a sword in his hands. The elk lowered his rack to spear the invader.

The general knew that he would have one chance to slay the beast. He just needed to get underneath its jaw to slit its throat. He didn't have enough power to kill it with a lightning blow to the heart. Ciardis scrambled up and dashed toward the two combatants. She couldn't do anything from here; the elk's magical protection was already going down, thanks to the verbane-laced arrow, and she didn't even know if she could attack it magically.

Barnaren glanced at her. His concentration had been broken by Ciardis's movement, and he quickly looked away. The elk reached him in that moment and Barnaren had to dodge to the side and under its angry hooves. It wasn't quite enough. His sword stroke missed, but as the stag raced past, it managed to spear the general's thigh with a tine. The tine snapped off in a clean break, but another immediately grew in its place.

The blood poison of the tines did its work within seconds. General Barnaren collapsed, unable to move his leg. His sword lay a few feet to one side.

The beast whirled on its hooves to finish off its now helpless opponent. In desperation, Barnaren scrambled across the ground, dragging his leg behind him as he reached for his sword. Making a spilt section decision Ciardis reached down and grabbed the sword first. She faced the elk.

"Ciardis, here," said the General in a harsh, pain-filled whisper behind her.

Turning to Barnaren, she stared at his outstretched hand for what seemed like a long moment before taking it. She had no idea what he was up to.

Baring his teeth in a grimace, he slammed his mage strength into hers. She realized that the poison was affecting not only his movement, but also his ability to practice magic. He was trying to save them both by giving her the power to defeat the elk.

But her magic didn't work like that, something the general suddenly understood. Swallowing quickly, she said, "Take my magic into you instead."

With no options left, he reversed the push into a pull and grabbed for her power in order to drain her core. Instantly, he felt a wealth of power—not from just Ciardis, but from the power she was pulling from the very earth beneath them. Taking what he could, he fashioned it into a spear of magic. A heavy arc of power raced from the general's hand to the white hart elk that was almost upon them now.

The bolt crashed into the middle of the beast's chest, and Ciardis saw the moment when its great heart stopped and the glimmer of life left its eyes. Before it had even crashed to the ground, its lifeblood had ceased to flow. Stone dead, the white hart elk skidded to a halt in the mud and grass near the edge of the little lake.

As it lay there silently, Ciardis turned once more to the general, and then looked down at their clasped hands. Taking a deep breath, she looked at his leg, noting the bone-white tine that protruded upright from the mangled mess of his thigh.

At that moment, she heard a voice call down from the ridge. When she looked up, she saw the general's guards cresting the ridge and scrambling down. She could see a healer in white rushing toward them.

"Thank you, Ciardis," the general gasped weakly. "Without your power, we would have both died."

"I only did what I have been trained to do – giving you the power," she responded.

"Nevertheless, in battle, the ones who win are those who can face their fears and get it done. You," he said, pausing to cough, "got it done."

The healer reached them and knelt to examine the torn leg. The healer ignored the beast behind him except for a cursory glance to determine that the material that impaled the general's leg was, in fact, a tine from the beast's rack. The healer then set to work. Moving with extreme care, he checked the tine's position—it had missed the great artery in the thigh—and then slowly pulled the tine from the bone with magical energy. It was a struggle, as the tine was awash with the magic of the beast, and he might not have accomplished it had Ciardis not reached out and grasped his hand. She quickly explained about her talent, and how she could strengthen the magic of other mages.

As he clutched her hand, his magic surged, and he was able to both remove the tine and combat the poison drifting in tendrils from it, cutting off the spread of the toxic vapors. After he'd tossed the neutralized tine aside, he cleansed the darkness from the general's body. Then, with a firm hand, he pushed the bones of the general's thigh back into place with a *snap*, and smoothed the torn muscles in his leg. The healer began working to fix the torn muscles like a sculptor with clay. Ciardis watched in fascination. She could actually see the healer's magic as he smoothed the frayed flesh and knitted the muscles and skin back together.

It was amazing.

Once his patient had returned from the brink of death, the healer met her eyes. "You have my thanks, Mistress Weathervane," he said gratefully. "He is past the critical stage now. We can take care of any other necessary treatments at the Healers Guild in Sandrin."

Turning to focus on Barnaren the healer said, "I need to put you in a healing sleep, milord, if you will permit it."

"Of course, Barthis. A moment, though." General Barnaren turned his head and told his second-in-command to take charge for the time being. She knew that General Barnaren was currently running a military campaign in the White Mountains. The basic knowledge had been passed to her as a part of his dossier. It was an important fact to note that his high-ranking role with the military meant he would often be away from his estates and therefore, her. If she signed a contract with him.

She wasn't sure if Barnaren was commanding his second-in-command to take charge of the Hunt or the military campaign itself. Before she could ask, the healer put a hand over General Barnaren's forehead and his eyes closed in slumber. Turning back to the task at hand the healer finished wrapping a dressing around the wound.

Barthis turned to look Ciardis straight in the eyes. "Without you, this would not have been possible. To do what I just did would have taken two healers, at least. I'm grateful," he said, bowing his head.

"You're welcome," said Ciardis. "I'm grateful you were here." They stood up and Barthis signaled to several guards to come forward. Two of the men who bore the insignia of Air mages began conferring with the healer.

"It's best to lift him with air. Keeping his body still and elevated at all times. Could you do this?" Barthis asked one of the Air mages.

"Yes," the Air mage confirmed. Ciardis watched as two other guards came forward to lift their commander and the Air Mages commanded the wind and the air to lift the General Barnaren from the arms of the guards. They made their way back up the hillside with the healer beside them.

Ciardis turned to their fallen foe, the beautiful white hart elk. Sighing, she knelt by its side. Except for the arrow piercing its ribs, it had no visible wounds; there was no sign of the lightning arc that had killed it on its soft white fur. Stifling a sob, she rested a hand on its cheek. After a moment she rose and made her way up the ridge on the heels of the guards.

CHAPTER THIRTEEN

As they walked through the forest, one of the guards brought a trumpet to his lips and blew a note, signaling all of the hunters. They reached the rest of the hunting party and mounted up to go back through the portal way.

Ciardis told Damias what had happened – from the time she went over the ridge until their meet up with the hunting party. "I practically killed the general myself," she said. "I'll never be a companion now. What kind of trainee gets their Patron candidate nearly killed? Serena will have me pack my bags the moment we return home."

Damias glanced anxiously over at the general, who lay sleeping between the two walking Air mages. His guards clutched their weapons nervously, as if they might be attacked at any moment. Damias bit his lip. "Nonsense," he said. "You didn't kill him; in fact, you saved his life, as only a Weathervane could have."

Ciardis smiled bitterly. "I'm not so certain everyone believes that." She looked over at Corporal SaBarnaren, who was riding at the front of their party, conversing with the healer on his left side with the general's counsel from Sandrin on his right.

Damias said, "Not to worry, my dear. We'll get this settled—and don't forget, your first Hunt ball is tonight!"

Joy, thought Ciardis with trepidation.

She listened with half a heart as the city came into view and several of the guards peeled back from their company under orders to retrieve the elk carcass for its pelt and to have the meat evenly divided between the General's house and the Companions' Guild.

When they reached the city and their company parted ways, Damias urged his horse into a canter up the racing thoroughfare with Ciardis following closely behind. Damias never let her ride on this street. The thoroughfare was known for fast traffic and lots of accidents involving the galloping messengers and nobility looking to show off. She knew he was worried then – the only reason he would use it would be to speed their travel back to the Companions' Guild. This street was set aside for fast-moving horses only; no carriages, wagons, or pedestrians were allowed. It was the ideal way to get through the city quickly.

When they reached their turnoff point near the Companions' Guild, they slowed their lathered horses to a sedate walk, and proceeded to move quietly through the crowds. It didn't take them long to reach their destination, though by then it was early evening and Lady Serena was pacing in the main hallway. *Maybe she already knows?* Thought Ciardis with some relief. *At least I won't have to tell her.*

That hope was dashed in the next moment when Serena threw up her hands screaming, "You're late! We have only two hours. *Two hours* to get you ready for the ball! You were supposed to be here hours ago."

Today just went from bad to worse.

Beside her, Damias sighed and said, "There's something you need to know, my dear Serena."

"Whatever it is can wait," snapped Serena. Her arms were crossed in front of her angrily, her delicate foot tapping impatiently on the flagstones.

Serena summoned a legion of hammam girls and started issuing orders. "Five of you are to go with Ciardis and prepare her for tonight. Use scented water. Her hair is to be combed and styled, her skin smooth, and her face made up." Serena turned to face the one hamman girl whose name she could remember, and that was only due to the brilliant nature of her hair – a flaming, bright red– Rose. "You are aware of the desired hair style?" Rose gave a swift nod. "Then get to work," said Serena with a dismissive wave.

Immediately, the women descended upon Ciardis and urged her towards the stairs leading down to the hammam. As she looked over her shoulder, Ciardis caught Damias's eye. With her eyes she pleaded with him. He gently took Serena's arm, directing her attention away from Ciardis, and began to explain in earnest what had happened at the Hunt and the delay that had almost cost them the general's life.

As Ciardis descended into the gloom, the heat of the steam bath rose to greet her. She was stripped of every article of clothing she wore. Huddling in the center of a pile of dirty clothes, she struggled to cover her private areas, mortified. The girls couldn't have cared less, of course. One stood behind her and untwisted the tight bun on the back of her head while pulling back the loose curls in her face until her hair fell around her face. Unweaving the strands, the girl set about combing it.

Another girl hustled her over to a large standing tub as the hairdresser scurried along behind her, still combing. Ciardis was urged into the tub, and after maneuvering her to their liking, the girls scrubbed and brushed until Ciardis's skin felt raw. Then, without warning, they pushed Ciardis under the water once, and then a second time. She came up spluttering, trying to get wet curls out of her face and the water out of her eyes.

As she stepped out of the tub a moment later, a girl with ginger hair began to rub a mixture of chestnut oil and lotion into her skin, making sure to knead it into every crease as if she were preparing bread for baking.

An hour later, Ciardis emerged from the baths primped and clean as she was handed off to the dressmaker and her minions.

She was soon standing in her bathrobe in the center of a large room, the center of a flurry of activity. When she'd arrived, Lady Serena had eyed her from head to toe, but hadn't acknowledged her otherwise. Serena now stood in the corner discussing something with the dressmaker.

Ciardis huddled miserably in the middle of the room while a girl applied the final touches to her hair, which was elaborately done in a beautiful mix of curls and thick, twisted braids on top of her head. The hairdresser had a difficult time with Ciardis's bouncing chestnut curls, but had managed to tame them for the evening. Ciardis eyed her reflection with happiness in the glass mirrors set on the wall.

On a pedestal before her was an orchid-purple dress, similar in make to those that the female companions wore to court functions, with gossamer sleeves and pearls knitted into the fabric. The skirt was loose enough for full, fast strides. Beside the dress stood two pairs of orchid-purple shoes; one set of proper heels with a high arch and slender clasps, the second more curious in design. The set that stood beside the heels were leather boots with a simple pattern stitched into the material.

Ciardis knelt down to look at both shoes as the dressmaker's assistant came up behind her. Smiling proudly, the girl—who couldn't have been more than fourteen—said, "The boots are for your Hunt."

"And the dress shoes?"

"For the dances, of course," was the dressmaker's assistant's amused reply.

Next the dressmaker came over with Serena walking behind her. They showed Ciardis a nook with a privacy screen in front for her to change. When she emerged she wore the radiant purple dress and the surprisingly comfortable purple heels. She was given drop pearl and amethyst earrings to match her dress, and allowed to keep the moonstone and sapphire anklet as long as it stayed hidden beneath her dress.

A few minutes later, Ciardis, Lady Serena, and Damias stepped into a large carriage on their way to the Duke of Carne's villa. "Well, Damias has told me about what happened on your blood hunt. I'm quite disappointed. To almost have the General die...we'll *never* hear the end of this. The gossip will be the talk of the imperial court for the whole season!" said Lady Serena sharply.

"But I—"

"No buts, no excuses. I had to ask Lady Vana to help me do a memory recall so that I could see exactly what happened. Do you know how much it cost me magically to draw up those ghostly images from so far away?"

"No, I—"

"No, you don't. You would not believe the bowing and scraping I've had to do before the Companions Council in the last hour! They wanted to end your prospective contract on the spot. Really, Ciardis, almost murdering a General, one of the brightest military minds of this era? And to top this horrible day off I've received word that Lord Kinsight has taken grave ill and will be withdrawing his petition entirely."

Ciardis shrunk in her seat, "I'm sorry about Lord Kinsight Serena but I could not have anticipated that or General Barnaren's actions. What did you want me to do? We went on the blood Hunt at your request. White hart elks are dangerous—surely you know that."

"What I do or do not know does not concern you," said Lady Serena. "What I expected was a small display of enhanced sportsmanship. An increase in the general's fire abilities or his inner strength would have been sufficient to make a good impression as a potential companion."

Ciardis pursed her lips, but didn't argue the subject further. *Even Serena has no idea what my powers are capable of. I couldn't just enhance a particular facet of his physical being; it had to be his inherent magical capability—fire is a major component of his battle strategy but his natural abilities clearly lie in producing lightning strikes.*

"What's done is done," said Serena, looking out the carriage window, anger still clearly etched on her face in the thin line of her pursed mouth and the unhappy glint in her eyes. "We still haven't figured out if this will damage your reputation, but we can't turn back now. I have no idea if General Barnaren will even attend upon you for the Patron Hunt now."

By this time, Ciardis was rapidly blinking her eyes to keep the moisture from slipping down her cheeks.

"Enough," said Damias. "She saved his life, and there's nothing that can be done to change what happened." Reaching over, he dabbed at Ciardis's eyes with a handkerchief and said, "No tears, dear—your makeup will run."

Nodding as she fought for control, Ciardis looked out the window to gather composure. On the hillside before them stood a magnificent mansion blazing with lights, carriages streaming in through the gated entrance. They had arrived at the Duke of Carne's villa. Ciardis schooled her face into an impassive mask and prepared to step out of the carriage into the cool night air.

She gathered her courage and left Serena and Damias. They would enter separately and wait for her inside the main ballroom. The fabric of her dress swept around her with a gentle glide as she approached the doors. The moment she entered the Great Hall, which overlooked the actual ballroom, Ciardis's stomach went aflutter. Young women and men, all potential companions or debutantes from noble families, milled about in the entrance hallway. Ciardis strode toward the center of the room. She knew no one in the room, and it was painfully obvious.

Where is Terris? She wondered.

Towards the front doors that led into the main ballroom, villa servants began to call out attendee names. As each person's name was called, they stepped forward and walked past her with fluid grace through the grand doors that led into the ballroom.

A butler called her name, and as she stepped forward, he informed her to prepare to be announced to the ballroom. As she moved toward the doors, the floor helpfully lit up beneath her feet. Her every step glowed momentarily before the light dissipated behind her. She halted in the entrance of the doorway, dress gleaming and every hair in place. The Master of Ceremonies announced her to the crowd gathered below.

"Ciardis Weathervane, daughter of the late Lady Amelia Lilian Weathervane, and companion Trainee of Lady Serena Projectoris."

Shoulders straight, Ciardis strode forward, passing through the door and descending the grand staircase. All eyes were on her.

Ciardis kept her eyes locked on Damias, who stood at the bottom of the long staircase, waiting to escort her through the main ballroom. As she reached him, he eased her left hand into the crook of his arm and proceeded to guide her to the steps of the raised dais where the Duke of Carne sat. When she reached the dais, she dipped into a curtsy, her dress pooling around her, her eyes on the floor.

"Rise," came the order from the man on the dais. "Lady Weathervane, it has been decades since I've had the pleasure of hosting a member of your family under my roof. In fact, the last was your beautiful mother."

Ciardis's breath caught in her throat. "You knew my mother, milord?"

"I did, indeed. Old age has its benefits. I can safely say that I was one of the few to have known your mother fairly well. She left court early on, as you know," he said with a laugh.

"No, milord, I was not aware."

The Duke grunted, "Well then, I have some stories to tell you."

As Ciardis stood, he looked over her head and gestured at the gathered courtiers. "But now is not the time. I must not neglect my other guests. You understand, of course?"

"Of course, milord," she murmured politely and dropped into a shallow curtsy. She turned to Damias and they walked away from the raised dais to join the gathered nobility and companions who stood on either side of the carpet.

After everyone had had the chance to mingle properly, the sound of a bell rang out in the grand ballroom. Two butlers came forward and began to expeditiously roll up the carpet. Ciardis looked to the dais and saw the Duke of Carne standing. He spoke to a man at his side who was draped in the long robes of a mage – the insignia on his breast looked like a horn of some kind. After they finished speaking the mage gestured outwards and Ciardis felt a wave of magic wash over the room.

When the Duke spoke to the crowd, his voice was amplified through the ballroom. *The mage beside him must have auditory powers,* she thought. "Welcome, ladies and gentlemen, to my villa. My wife and I are pleased to welcome so many distinguished guests this evening. Tonight's festivities will feature a debut dance and a

Mordair maze challenge."

At that announcement, the man nearest Ciardis turned to his partner and whispered, "This Hunt will be even better than the last."

Ciardis wasn't surprised at the palpable excitement; the Patron Hunt was one of the most highly anticipated events of the year. The nobles came not only for the opportunity to assess future companions and marriage partners, but also for the entertainment of watching young mages compete against each other in exciting tasks.

"This is the first night of the Hunt, which will be followed by one more night and two days," the Duke said.

Ciardis's hand was tense on Damias's arm. "If you thought a blood hunt was bad, surely a Mordair maze is a worse idea," she whispered.

As they headed to the wine table, Damias responded, "Serena and I anticipated this challenge. What we did not anticipate was the General taking on the white hart elk with just you and absent his guards."

Ciardis, who was sipping on a glass of blueberry dessert wine, nearly choked at the censure. "Not unexpected? Are you saying that you knew that I would face this maze challenge tonight? Why didn't you inform me? I came here to *dance* not to race against my life."

"The maze will not be difficult – more of a test of your cleverness rather than your magic."

"I don't suppose you plan on telling me about the activities for the next two days and tomorrow night, then?" she said, sarcasm dripping from her lips.

"I planned to do so tonight," he responded. "The first night's activities are required by Guild law to be kept secret from the trainees until formally announced. The following day's activities can be explained upon the first night's conclusion."

Ciardis frowned unhappy with the decision.

"Don't worry, my dear," he said. "The Guild has well prepared you for the tasks you will come across. Just think clearly and be brave."

Then the orchestra began a set, and the music filtered throughout the room with excellent clarity due to the help of the auditory mage.

Behind Ciardis and Damias a person cleared their throat.

Ciardis turned, sipping the dark wine, and was surprised to see a young woman with her hands clasped anxiously. She wore brilliant blue mage robes with golden scrollwork stitched into the fabric.

Damias excused himself to greet a friend he saw off to right.

Ciardis smiled and dipped into a gentle curtsy; her orchid dress spread out smoothly around her like flower petals.

The girl responded with a short bow and a shy smile. "My name is Mina."

"Ciardis. A pleasure to meet you."

"I had heard about your amazing powers, and wanted to come over to introduce myself."

Ciardis smiled. "How sweet of you. It's always a chore to find someone to chat with at a party. I'm happy I don't have to go through those awkward introductions that no one likes. I can tell you're a mage, but I'm at a loss as to what kind."

"Oh," said Mina, a hint of a blush on her cheeks. "I'm an auditory mage. I'm usually working with the orchestra during the evening dances, but my father—a sonorous mage—took my place so that I could attend the ball."

Ciardis's eyes widened in excitement. "He's a sonorous mage? I've never met one of those."

Mina turned to gaze at a dancing couple in the ballroom, then turned back to Ciardis. "It's the second level for an auditory mage, which is what I am. There are different type of mage powers connected to sound and sight. As a first-level auditory mage I can amplify sound in both closed and open settings, but I have a limited range. My father, who has advanced to the level of sonorous mage, can amplify a general's orders across a battlefield, if needed."

"That's impressive."

"Yes," Mina said. "I hope to be as capable one day. You're here to find a patron, yes?"

Ciardis nodded. "Yes, I'm pretty excited to meet with my prospective patrons – or at least the other ones."

The girl nodded her head, "It must be so exciting to meet marriage partners like that. Hopefully you get a brilliant match."

"Life partners," corrected a familiar voice from behind them.

Mina and Ciardis turned in surprise. Prince Sebastian, in his role as Viscount Iskas of Marce, stood before them in his court robes. Smiling, he stepped forward and took Mina's hand in his and gave her hand a light kiss. "A pleasure to meet you, milady."

She blushed profusely before returning his greeting. As Sebastian turned to Ciardis, she couldn't help but note the mischief in his eyes. With a teasing smile, he said, "Debutantes come looking for marriage partners, while companions come for life partners. After all, no one ever said that marriage had to be forever."

Ciardis noted that while Mina seemed a trifle flustered it wasn't the excitement that would come with meeting a Prince but rather a handsome gentleman.

Sebastian must be wearing that bracelet again, she thought a trifle annoyed. She took a peek at his wrist but his robes extended to below his cuffs.

Mina stifled a giggle, but was otherwise unfazed. "He's right, Ciardis. My father has been married four times, but has kept the same mistress for twenty years."

Ciardis raised an eyebrow at Mina.

"Not that I'm saying a companion is anything like a mistress,"

Mina hastily said while looking horrified.

Ciardis laughed. "I don't mind. In Vaneis, we called a stork a stork and a dog a dog. The only difference between a companion and a mistress is that the Companions' Guild tends to accept only magic users as opposed to marriage which looks for social and class compatibility."

Sebastian, still posing as Viscount Marce, said, "Some would say the magical qualities that make a companion so interesting make a world of difference."

He bowed smoothly and then straightened, looking at Ciardis and gesturing to the dance floor. She looked hesitantly at Mina; she didn't want to leave her standing alone. The girl quickly shooed her away, and as Ciardis headed to the dance floor on Sebastian's arm, she saw Damias approach Mina for a dance. Ciardis mouthed, "*Thank you,*" to him as she stepped onto the ballroom floor.

CHAPTER FOURTEEN

The Prince Heir didn't waste any time. "Have you made a decision?" he asked.

As they whirled across the dance floor, Ciardis asked coyly, "Have you, my Prince?"

"Have I what?"

Ciardis sighed; he was such a child. "What exactly are you asking for?" she said.

"I've spent some time researching the Algardis legends with an expert, and—"

"Which expert?" she interrupted.

"An older gentleman with a distinguished service record."

"A mage?" she said.

"Well, no, he works as a building architect," he admitted.

When she raised an eyebrow, he amended his statement, adding, "An architect of the summer palace for the Imperial children. But he knows quite a lot about Imperial history—his mother was the court librarian, and he says that to unlock my tie to the land, we have to convince the Land Wight to reinstate my connection to the land on the night of the winter solstice."

"That's tonight," Ciardis said faintly.

"I know," Sebastian said. For a few moments, his hands tightened on her waist, and his tone grew dark when he spoke again. "But this is my only chance. I can only gain access to the Land Wight in the Aether Realm once a year, otherwise we must take the chance that he will appear at a land ceremony which hasn't happened in years."

Ciardis looked up at him and saw him as he was: a young man, on the cusp of adulthood, uncertain and determined at the same time. *The rumors about him can't be true. He obviously cares not just for himself but for the Empire as a whole.*

Putting aside her doubts she said, "I have already sworn my aid, but we need a plan."

"I have one. Meet me at the maze's end three hours before dawn," he said.

She almost objected, but didn't quite know what to object to. He stopped their dance, and to Ciardis's surprise, Lord SaBarnaren cut in.

"My father wanted this conveyed to you personally," he said as dispassionately as possible, the frost in his eyes showing what he truly felt. "He bears you no ill will for your hesitation in the forest."

SaBaranen's eyes were fascinating to look at—frost swirled around his eyelids and cold emanated from his touch. He wasn't fighting to control the physical symptoms of his powers – allowing it to leak. It was a deliberate slap in the face to Ciardis. Mages were not supposed to leak their gifts in any form without express reason.

He paused for a long moment, then said, "In fact, he considers your courage and tenacity to be ideal qualities for a strong companion and future wife. He would be pleased to continue his candidacy as a prospective Patron." This last bit he spit out with all the rancor of someone who had eaten spoiled meat.

Ciardis smiled. "The general has my gratitude."

"I'm sure he does."

They drifted apart as the dance ended. Over the course of the evening, Ciardis partnered with a couple more young gentlemen, occasionally catching the eye of Serena or Damias, who would nod and smile to indicate that she was doing well. *Just a little more dancing—a few more waltzes,* she kept telling herself.

When the time came to enter the Maze of Mordair, she was relieved.

Every companion trainee left the ballroom when the clock struck eleven. As they left the ballroom and entered a hallway servants directed them to rooms set aside for them. In hers Ciardis found breeches, a tunic, a knapsack, a belt, and a hunting knife waiting for her on the bed, with her purple boots sitting on the floor.

She put everything on and shouldered the knapsack. She couldn't take her elaborately coiffed hair down without help, so she decided to leave it as it was.

As soon as she finished dressing, on the far wall a panel swung open. She heard a faint *pop* as she passed through the dark doorway— the same pop she'd felt when she'd gone through the portal way to the elk hunt. She felt uncertainly in the darkness around her and found sturdy walls to her left and right.

Unsure of where she was going but still pressing forward she strode ahead carefully, wary of steps or sudden dips. After a few minutes, which felt like hours in the dark, claustrophobic tunnel, Ciardis ran into a wall that was rough with the texture of dirt and the scraggly feel of roots. She began to panic, frantically feeling along its surface until she found a raised knob in the center. Hoping against hope, she turned it.

The door opened outward onto a well-lit grassy plain. Though it was quite dark, plenty of light shone down from the moon and the bevy of mage orbs floating overhead. Ah, so this was the Maze of Mordair! Tall, dark-green hedges towered above her on every side, denser than any she had ever seen before and three times the height of a tall man. She knew that she could not climb over or fight her way through the hedge walls. In front of her stood the opening to the maze.

As she moved forward into the open area, she heard what sounded like doors opening on either side of the one she had come out of. The other companion trainees stepped out of their own changing areas. They glanced at each other and began to assess the area. Once they had all come to the same conclusion—that there was nowhere to go and nothing to do—they gathered in the center open area.

Ciardis barely had time to acknowledge Terris with a grin and a nod before the sounds of swift wings beating in the night came close overheard.

A man descended out of the sky. He had a wingspan to rival that of the winged horses and the white hair and pale skin of the angelic Ansari race. He cupped his wings and landed in their midst.

"Please gather around," he said. The companion trainees came forward to surround him in a half circle.

"Welcome, Kardin, Ciardis, Samantha, Terris, and Brandon, to the first night of your Patron Hunt. You have each been judged for your skills in the ballroom tonight, and it is now time to assess your ability to maneuver and think intelligently during the Hunt."

"Although some of us have already been partially assessed on that front," he said with a lingering gaze on Ciardis.

Oh no…he can't mean me! Ciardis thought with dread back on her problems with the blood hunt.

"And done quite well I might add," he continued before he returned his attention back to the full group.

Well, that's a relief...if he meant me.

"The practicality of your abilities as well as your solutions to problems encountered in the maze will be noticed and weighed," he continued. "I will be flying a dedicated route above the maze along with two other Ansari. We will watch over you from the skies but will not interfere unless summoned. Your progress will also be carefully monitored by a panel of our distinguished patron guests and mentors who accompanied you to the villa."

"An orb awaits each of you at the end of the maze," he said. "Whoever reaches their orb first will receive the highest score. A range of points may be deducted depending on the length of time it takes you to reach the end and the way in which you confront your obstacles. Each orb is spelled to the color of your boots, so you will know which is yours."

Ciardis quickly took a peek at the feet of the other companion trainees. She saw red, yellow, blue, and green boots – all with the same simple pattern woven into them. But only she wore purple boots.

Which means my orb will be purple.

"The boots also track your location in the maze. If you feel that you are in imminent danger, you may touch the boots with your hand to request an immediate rescue. But if you do so, you forfeit all points in this test." He looked up at them. "Is this understood?"

They nodded.

The Ansari stepped back, spread his wings and took off into the sky. As he hovered, he waved his hand at the maze opening, and a barrier protecting the entrance of the maze dissipated in front of them. "Begin!" he shouted.

They took off at a run and were immediately met with three paths. Dividing up they followed the path their instincts led them to. Ciardis was sure there was one other trainee behind her, but with all the twists and turns and openings in the maze, she soon lost track of him.

As she rounded a corner in the maze, she came face to face with a pit viper the size of an elephant. Pale with fear, Ciardis backed away slowly. Only a fool wouldn't have expected surprises in the maze, but a deadly serpent that could swallow her whole had not been on her list of possibilities.

She gulped and kept her eyes on it, waiting for it to slither forth and strike, but it didn't move a scaly muscle. It just kept its glaring red eyes trained on her. She'd backed up against the maze wall by this time, and began inching backward with the maze wall to her left. As soon as she hit the corner, she took off with her heart in her throat. She had no illusions that she could out distance the serpent, but saw no other choice.

While glancing over her shoulder for a hint of red eyes in the darkness behind her, she ran so fast in fright that she slammed into another person. They both crashed to the ground on opposite sides of the corridor, a glow orb tumbling to the ground beside the stranger. Groaning, they were both back on their feet in seconds. She recognized the gorgeous features of Brandon, one of the two male trainees in the Hunt.

"Run! We have to go back!" said Ciardis. "There's a giant serpent around the corner!"

"We can't," the boy said. "The wall shield at the front of the maze is back up – there's no way back out – only through the maze."

Ciardis quickly jogged back toward the maze entrance to check for herself. Sure enough, there was no path back. She uttered a choice oath.

When she ran back to Brandon, she found that he'd extended the light of his orb a fair distance in front of them. She set her pack down and began rummaging in it. "What are you doing?" he asked, bringing the orb closer.

"Keep the light trained on the path ahead of us! We need the light there – at least we'll see it coming. I can see in the pack well enough with the light I have."

He nodded and went back to watching for any sign of the serpent's eyes or scales glinting in the light. Meanwhile, Ciardis stared at the contents of her knapsack, which were now spread out on the ground before her. She had a rope, but no grappling hook; water, but no food; gold dust, but no coins; a sharp blade and what looked like a small, blank notebook. Brandon asked her what she'd found, and she rattled off the list of contents. After a quick check, he acknowledged the same contents in his own knapsack.

Ciardis was faintly irritated with the lack of usable goods, but decided to see if she could fashion a loop out of the rope. *Maybe we could use it to get a grip on the top of the hedge and climb over.* She tried it once, twice, but no luck. There was a barrier blocking the top of the hedge; it seemed that the organizers of the Patron Hunt didn't want any of the companion trainees climbing over it.

She stood up, pondering their next step. "I haven't seen any monsters, snakes or otherwise," Brandon said.

Ciardis eyed the path back towards the serpent uneasily. "Well, that serpent is there. Just around the bend."

Taking a deep breath, Brandon strode forward. She could see him turn two shades paler as he looked around the corner, and he hastily backed away from the corner where he presumably saw the serpent, and back towards her. "Yeah, it's there," he said.

"What was it doing?"

"Sitting on its coils with its head tucked at the top, ready to strike."

"In order to strike, it has to move at some point. That's the same position it was in when I was there. Hmm."

They looked at each other and then back at the corner. Together they approached the turn again; this time, they were prepared for the glittering red eyes. "It's not moving," he said. "Not at all."

"No, it hasn't," she agreed. They walked out in full view of the serpent. It remained coiled, staring. Frowning, the boy held his orb higher and increased the burst of light. When the light hit the snake's eyes, they glittered with the brilliance of gemstones. Ciardis gasped in awe, "The eyes look like gemstones! Rubies maybe?"

"It's not real, then?"

"I don't think so," she said uncertainly.

Shouldering their packs, they walked forward, close to the maze's edge, as if that might somehow protect them. As they crept by the serpent statue, where there was about eight feet of space between the wall and its coils, they held their breath, hoping it wasn't a real snake in a stasis spell and especially hoping that it wouldn't suddenly come to life before their eyes.

They hit an invisible barrier of air on the serpent's left side, and nearly soiled themselves when they couldn't get around. After some exploring on the other side, they determined that the serpent still wasn't moving, but neither could they get around it.

They looked at each other and back at the serpent. Ciardis decided that enough was enough. Too much time had passed trying to get around it. She walked straight up to the still serpent and look at it carefully.

"I don't think it's ever going to do anything," she said over her should to Brandon. He moved forward to touch the green scales glowing in the moonlight. "It *looks* real but the scales are as hard as stones."

"So it's just a statue then?"

"Maybe," he replied while looking for markings or writings to indicate it was an automaton – a machine imbued with magic which would give it lifelike qualities. It hadn't moved once so maybe it was made out of stone – like a statue.

The boy squinted at the serpent's head. "Huh. I think there's something up there."

Some kind of slender, short pole was jutting out of the top of the statue's head.

"Yeah," Ciardis agreed cautiously. "Think we can climb over then?"

"As long as the barrier doesn't extend over its head," he said.

"Alright then, I think if we tie both of our ropes together and lasso that pole, we can use it as an anchor point to climb up the statue," she said.

Seeing no other way forward, they went forward with the plan. Brandon turned out to be good with a lasso, catching the pole with the noose on his first try. They struggled up and over, and as they dropped down to the other side, a deadly hiss split the stillness of the night behind them.

They didn't bother collecting their ropes or turning around. Hearts in their throats, they ran.

Twenty steps past the serpent, just before they turned a corner, they hit another glimmering barrier. Ciardis stepped through first. When she turned around Brandon was gone and the barrier had turned opaque – she couldn't see the path back from where she came.

But she wasn't alone, she soon realized. On this new side of the barrier sat an old crone with wrinkled skin, beady eyes, baggy clothes, and fey fluttering around her. Ciardis wrinkled her nose; she didn't smell very nice.

"Well, my daughter you have passed your first test," the crone croaked. "You stood up to the serpent and faced your fear."

Ciardis gave her a smile. The ancient one cackled, "I know your thoughts, young one; I've read your fears. It's time to prove to yourself and to me that you're more than just a pretty face. Pretty faces we have plenty of; keen minds are harder to find."

Ciardis approached her cautiously, until she stood five steps from the old woman, just out of reach of her knotted cane. She did not want to get whacked with that stick; the wood looked strong enough to break bones with a single blow.

This woman could give the Old Mothers of the village who stayed in the common space day after day and harassed everyone who walked by, lessons in acidity. She curtsied and asked respectfully, "What would you like to know, then, Old Mother?"

The woman smiled at what she presumed was an honorific, revealing gruesome, decayed gums with five yellowed teeth haphazardly placed. Only Ciardis's training kept her from visibly flinching. "Let's play a game, then, shall we, my dear?"

Seeing no other choice, Ciardis nodded her head in reluctant acceptance.

"One is blue, the other is green, but only for a moment in the lakes unseen, changing colors and tails aglow, they hide in plain sight with the colors below. Tell me, young weathervane, what is it I've seen?" the crone crooned.

A riddle. Two forms, two bodies? No—two forms, same body. Because they have changing colors and tails that glow. But they live in lakes...and hide in plain sight?

She paced before the old crone, the woman's cackling hurting her ears. Ciardis looked up and grimaced; an hour had passed so far, and it was already midnight. *Two hours until the contest ends, and three hours until I have to meet Sebastian at the maze's end,* she thought glumly, *and I can't even decipher this old lizard's riddle.*

Something itched in the back of her mind as soon as she thought "lizard." *With the colors below,* she wondered, mystified. *Below what? Below...the surface!*

"That's it!" she said with a gleeful clap of her hands, turning back to face the seated woman. "A water salamander! They change colors to blend in and live in lakes."

A frown spread across the crone's face, but she grudgingly nodded, "You've solved my riddle and passed this portion of the Mordair maze."

As Ciardis prepared to race off, the woman halted her.

"One more thing, young woman: you'll face two more challenges ahead. But I believe you have something in your bag that's mine." she said.

"What would that be?" Ciardis asked.

The woman held out her hand and rubbed the tips of her fingers together in the universal sign for money. Ciardis couldn't believe her gall, but she supposed that that was what the gold dust was for.

As she raced off with her pack two items lighter, she heard the old crone's cackle echoing through the maze behind her.

CHAPTER FIFTEEN

As Ciardis advanced, a dark mist began to flood the pathway. She stumbled forward into a clearing and turned to look behind her. The mist had condensed into a solid wall. *Not that I'd want to go back that way,* she mused.

She examined her options. The path split in a V, and neither offshoot had any characteristics distinguishing one from the other. She looked up and groaned aloud. The moon was even higher in the sky. She didn't have much time left to finish her tasks.

Then, still staring upward she saw something. She could have sworn she'd seen something winged flying above her; and then it passed in front of the moon, its bright light outlining a human figure against the outline of its waning curve. Whoever it was, they were clearly struggling. The Ansari man wouldn't be flying so erratically over the maze. Deciding it might be Samantha, who was half-Ansari, she let out a long, piercing whistle and called the girl's name.

As the figure flew closer and the red hair whipping behind her became visible, Ciardis could tell that it was definitely the spitfire from the Winged Isles. But something was wrong. Ciardis stared up intently. *Why is she flying so low?* Samantha's pattern was erratic, and she was coming in too forcefully—far too fast to manage a graceful landing. Ciardis rapidly backed away in order to clear space in the corridor.

Samantha managed to right herself enough that she could land vertically but even Ciardis could see she was out of breath and looked exhausted. She hunched over, hands on her knees, as she tried to catch her breath. "Hey, relax," said Ciardis as she approached the wheezing girl. She gave Sam her bottle of water, hoping it would help.

Raising her head Samantha gave Ciardis a tired smile as she drank some of the water.

"My mage core depleted more rapidly than it ever has," Samantha explained. "I've never needed to use so much magic to fly such a short distance before. I've had to stop every few minutes in the maze to regain a little strength."

She ruffled her wings in the same way a human shake their shoulders to brush off a weird feeling, "There are some bad things in this maze. Once I barely escaped from a chimera hiding in the shadows." Samantha rubbed her stiff shoulders, wincing.

"Think you can make a fewer more miles?" Ciardis asked, "The maze end can't be too far off."

"I could but it'll take too long - my wind strength and flight ability are tied to my mage power. The stronger my reserve of power, the higher, the longer, and the faster I can fly," Samantha explained.

Ciardis took a swig of water herself. "Tell you what: I'll help you fly, and you can get us to the end of the maze."

Samantha eyed her curiously. "What do you mean?"

"I mean if you can carry me, I can give you the mage power necessary to fly us both. That's my talent: I enhance other mage talents."

Samantha decided that at this point, she didn't have much to lose. "All right, let's do this," Samantha said. "You're as tall as I am, so carrying you in my arms is out. You'll have to hop on my back." At Ciardis's raised eyebrow, Samantha said, "It'll be an awkward flight, but it's the only way it'll work – unless you have an expanding basket in your backpack *and* can enhance without physical contact."

That's an interesting point. Could I enhance a mage's abilities without touching them? I was holding hands with both General Barnaren and Sebastian when I enhanced them. I'll have to test it out later.

Not wasting any more time, Samantha squatted down and Ciardis hopped onto her back. Ciardis felt Samantha's lagging flight power through her skin and immediately tapped into her own well of power to boost it. Just before they lifted off, Ciardis said, "Let's not ever mention this to anyone, agreed?"

Samantha quickly said, "Agreed."

Then they raced into the sky, Ciardis's power giving Samantha the push she needed to fly strong. They quickly spotted the end of the maze and headed toward the clearing with the glowing orbs in the center.

When they were within a few dozen feet of the maze's exit, a beam of light shot out of the ground and struck Sam in the chest. They tumbled toward the ground, screaming. Ciardis's heart was in her throat—and her stomach wasn't far behind—as she imagined broken bones and torn skin when their bodies smashed into the ground.

But fifty feet from the ground, they began to slow; air was funneling under them and cushioning their fall. The wind power wasn't coming from either girl. In fact it seemed to emanate from the maze itself. Their descent wasn't as hectic as before, but it was still fast. They landed with a dizzying *thump*. Ciardis checked her body for injuries, but noted no broken bones. She reached over to

Samantha, who lay curled on the ground almost as if she were sleeping.

Ciardis leaned over her friend and tried shaking her awake. A quick glance didn't reveal any bones sticking out at odd angles; there was no blood pooling under her body, and even her wings were their normal shape.

Samantha awoke. "Wha' happened?" she muttered groggily, clutching her head in her hands as she struggled to a sitting position.

"Don't know. A beam of light shot up from the ground and hit you. When it did, we went down. But something caught us before we hit the ground too hard."

"Dammit," cursed Samantha. "Guess it couldn't be that easy, could it?"

"At least we're closer to the end than when we started."

"True."

They stood up and immediately Samantha crumbled back to the ground clutching her waist. She was cursing so much Ciardis couldn't understand what was wrong.

"God, my ribs," Samantha said. Kneeling next to her Ciardis hovered helplessly.

"What do you want me to do?"

"I don't know," said Sam. "It hurts to breathe. I need a medic. You'd better go."

"But –" Ciardis said.

"There's no reason for *both* of us to get caught," Sam said.

They were both aware of the unspoken rule that companion trainees should do no more than what was necessary to help each other, and they were never to team up for any reason.

Ciardis looked around - she couldn't see the end of the maze but knew they were close. *Close enough to help Sam hobble to the end?* She didn't think so. To top it off Ciardis's left leg was stiff from the fall, and every time she stretched it, she felt a pain in her upper muscle.

Grimacing, she massaged her thigh; she guessed that she'd probably pulled the muscle. Samantha saw the pained expression, "Enough. Just go – I'm calling in help." Ciardis nodded and hobbled towards an opening in the maze wall. It'd be best to get into the shadows of its overhang before help arrived. She turned back for a few seconds to see Samantha touching her yellow boot in a summons for aid.

That short flight bought me the time I needed. If I'm correct, I just need to make two lefts and a right and I'll be through the maze.

She hobbled forward, but sighed in irritation when she reached the first corner. Before her was a dark pond that filled the entire maze corridor. She briefly considered turning back, but knew that this was the fastest - and perhaps the only way - for her to get through.

She also knew that there was probably something nasty in or around the pond.

She tested the water and immediately determined that the depth was substantially greater than she'd first thought. Crouching down, she noticed an inscription in the mud beside the pond water.

A mirage is only as real as you make it.

In thought, she flicked her eyes back over the depths. Could it all be a mirage? Taking a hesitant step forward and telling herself firmly that the water was just a hallucination of her imagination, she planted a purple boot in the loose mud of the pond. She drew back hastily as she felt water raise up her foot. For a few seconds the sucking mud had felt like it was trying to drag her down. Scrambling further back from the edge, she tried to decide what to do next.

Maybe the knapsack contains the key, she thought. Rummaging through it, she found that besides the water bottle, she only had the notebook left. Somehow, it would have to do. Opening it, she leafed through the pages, looking for a clue. Nothing appeared on the ruled leaves…and then, as she prepared to close the book, a glint flashed in her eyes. She stared down at the notebook, more intensely this time.

It was as if magic were coruscating off the page.

Now, there was an intriguing thought. *Could the notebook be imbued with magic, perhaps even a casting spell of some kind, like a Residual Magic object?* She thought fleetingly of her—well, Sebastian's—anklet. Removing the built-in stylus from the notebook's spine, she began drawing on the flickering page, first sketching the pond and then the maze hedges surrounding it. She looked up hopefully, but nothing had happened. On a whim, she drew a small tree, and gasped in awe as a replica appeared in the corresponding spot on the other side of the pond in front of her.

The pond and hedges were already there. But the tree *wasn't*. She'd found the key.

Biting her lip and concentrating, she began to draw stepping-stones across the pond's surface. She wasn't much of an artist, but stepping-stones were easier to draw than a bridge. As quickly as she drew them, they appeared. Ciardis stepped lightly onto the stone nearest her; it held, so she raced across the pond, drawing more and more stones until she reached the far edge.

Sighing in relief, she turned back to face the pond. After staring at it for a long moment, she decided to leave the notebook at the water's lapping edge as a tribute, just as the rope and gold dust had been. Just before she set the notebook down, writing appeared on the page in a heavy script.

Excellently done, Ciardis. Your imaginative solution has served you well. Proceed.

She turned and hobbled as fast as she could down the maze corridor. As she rounded the second to last corner, she slowed, thinking unhappily, *Running across that pond did my leg no good.* She hoped a healer would be waiting for the contestants at the maze's end.

For the next few minutes, she encountered nothing—and then she saw it. The exit stood at the end of the corridor, and beyond that, her purple orb hovered in the center of the clearing. She hurried forward, and as she reached the landing just before the outer doorway, a shape appeared out of thin air. *Rats*, she thought, *I'd hoped I'd skipped over a task by riding on Samantha's back. If I had the deep pond would have been my last obstacle. Apparently not.*

She came to a halt before the figure. It had no face, and was cloaked head to foot in a metallic golden robe that rippled in the moonlight. "Ciardis Vane," it said in a sonorous voice. "You wish to be acknowledged as a Weathervane—a mage of immense Innate Magic—and a companion—one who has the potential to shatter the Imperial Court."

Ciardis paled. "I—"

"I am the Oracle," it said. "I do not state opinions, merely facts."

"Yes sir," she said quietly.

"I am neither sir nor ma'am to you," it corrected. "I will ask you a question, and you will answer honestly. You stand on an abandoned road, alone, and miles from the nearest village. A child approaches you, one without magic. He has been maimed; he only has one arm. He says he has been expelled from his home and his village. The village headman says he is useless and should die on the road. What would you say?"

Ciardis lifted her head and said fiercely, "No one is useless—*no one.* There will always be a task, a skill, a gift that the boy has that no one else can do. I would tell the boy this, then offer him anything I had to ease his way including coins, food and a warm hearth to lay down beside."

The oracle continued without acknowledging her response. "Two days later, the boy steals your purse. He holds a knife to your throat and you see fear cloud his eyes. He says, 'I can't trust you. I can't trust anyone. I'm sorry.' He leaves with your valuables. What would you say to him if you could?"

Her voice steady, Ciardis said, "I would wish him well on his journey, because nothing in that pack is worth his life or mine. I would tell him to drink the water sparingly, because the next village is miles away and the dry heat will leave him parched."

For a full minute, the oracle said nothing. Then it stated, "Very well, Ciardis Weathervane. You have passed. Proceed."

She walked past the Oracle. Dark hedges arose to her left and right and the path ahead was dusted with fallen red leaves strewn over the dirt. She could see the clearing ahead and the moonlight shining down from the round orb lighting her path. Just before she stepped out of the maze, Ciardis turned and reached into her knapsack. She held out the water bottle and asked, "Is it yours?"

The Oracle did not turn, but replied, "No, child—it is yours."

Ciardis kept the water and hobbled toward her orb. She saw that she wasn't the last to arrive, thank goodness; the green orb hovered nearby. The yellow orb, Samantha's, lay unmoving on the ground. Reaching for the purple, she carefully palmed it. She could tell upon touching it that there was an activation switch on the side.

As she prepared to flip the switch, a sharp whistle pierced the air.

Turning to her left, she saw Sebastian standing off to the side. He gestured for her to come into the shadows. "What?" she snapped. "I have another half hour. I need to flip the switch on the side of this orb – it will notify the judges that I've completed the maze. I would *prefer* to do that before the last contestant grabs their orb."

She looked anxiously over at the green orb to ensure that it was still there.

"I was wrong about the time. I—*we*—miscalculated the time of the winter equinox by twenty minutes. It's sooner than I thought. We have to go now!"

"Alright. Let's go then," she said while moving to flip the orb's activation switch.

"No! If you flip that switch, it'll transport you directly to the winner's hall." He reached out a hand. "Here, I can activate the panel so the judges will know you've made it to the end of the maze and you don't disappear on me."

Frowning, she handed over the orb.

After a few quick seconds when he poked the orb, a panel on its side lit up. "Touch the panel," he said. She rested her palm on it, and a message that read, "*Completed*," began to scroll across the surface. "There," he said. "Now, come on."

"Wait, there's something else," she said, remembering the ache in her leg.

As he looked at her with impatience, she explained, "I hurt my leg. I can't run."

Swiftly, he knelt down and eyed the cloth wrapped around her leg. Carefully, he prodded the tender muscles beneath the bandage with gentle fingertips. "What are you doing?" she whispered.

"I can heal small things," he said, concentrating. "Broken fingers, small bruises, little cuts." Looking back up at her with a wicked smile, he said, "Comes with the territory of being semi-connected to the land. Otherwise I could heal a person at the brink of death." He touched her leg once more and stood up.

She gave the leg a test shake. The pain was gone. Flashing him a vivacious smile, she said, "Looks like you're good for something after all, Prince Sebastian."

He snorted in amusement and said, "Glad to be of service, milady," and they proceeded to move out, Ciardis following close behind him.

CHAPTER SIXTEEN

As they strode into the forest, a distant bell tolled the half hour. "We're late," she said anxiously.

"No, we're right on time." Grabbing her hand, Sebastian activated the residual magic of the ankle bracelet she wore with a small push of his power. Her stomach twisted as she felt the two of them jump.

They returned to the Aether Realm.

When they materialized in the strange place in between the heavens and earth, they were at the base of a mountain—a mountain Ciardis recognized. Huge twin peaks looked in the distance that were also familiar – the White Mountains of the North. As she turned in a circle to get her bearings, she eyed their surroundings with growing recognition. The trees, the vegetation, even the path was familiar to her. They were on the trail of a minor vale near Vaneis. She'd hiked out here many times to gather her thoughts, and obtain the plants she needed to create her special red dye mix.

When she turned around, Prince Sebastian was already heading up a worn mountain trail that she could barely see in the dark. A couple of light orbs appeared in the air in front of him and one floated back to her.

The entrance to the mountain was located on the southwest slope of Varis Mountain, in the valley of Varis itself. Vaneis was on the other side of the mountain; this was the barrier separating the two communities. "You don't want to head that way," she called urgently.

"Why not?" he said as his voice drifted back to her.

She stumbled, stubbing her toe, and cursed quietly as she hurried to catch up to the light. "Because," she said reluctantly, "it's haunted."

Even in the darkness, she could read the mocking expression on his face as he looked back at her. "It is," she insisted.

"I don't believe in things being haunted."

"Well, I don't believe in Land Wights, and yet here am I."

He shushed her when they reached the mountainside entrance and she punched him on the shoulder in irritation. *The nerve of the brat, shushing me like that!*

"Whatever orders I give you, from now until we leave this mountain, you must follow without question," he said urgently. She hesitated. "Ciardis!" he said holding up his hand as she began to protest. "The mountain isn't inhabited by a ghost, but rather an elemental trapped between the Aether Realm and the mortal realm. It manifests here, but it knows nothing of leniency or mercy. It knows the codes and the blood, that's all."

She gritted her teeth and said, "The codes and the blood?"

"My blood," he said, "and the correct answers, which will allow passage to its grotto."

When they reached the entrance to the mountain, he took off his pack and motioned for her to do the same. Armed with a small knife at her waist, she followed the Prince Heir through the stone doorway and into the pitch darkness. Sebastian produced a third light orb from his pocket, gave it a shake, and set it floating above their heads along with the other orbs illuminating the way.

They followed a twisted path with walls that felt like they were closing in and stalactites that dripped constantly, filling the air with the echoes of water splashing into lightless pools. Otherwise there was silence, save for the scuff of their feet and the occasional whisper of the wind through the small branching tunnels. Before long, they came to an open hole in the ground, though Ciardis thought that calling it a "hole" was being generous. It was really just a crack with rounded edges. "Here we are," Sebastian said cheerfully. "We'll be going down this ladder."

"Ladder?" Ciardis peered down into the darkness. "What ladder?"

"There are small notches chiseled into the stone wall," he said.

Ciardis looked at him like he'd gone insane. "That hole is barely big enough for either of us to fit into!"

"Which is why we left the knapsacks behind," he said patiently.

Ciardis sighed. "How far down does this go?"

"Only about fifteen feet, from what I remember." At her scowl, he said defensively, "It's been ten years since I've been here!"

Ciardis couldn't argue with that. "What's at the bottom?"

"A straight tunnel off to the left."

"What's to the right?"

"An invisible drop-off into a bottomless chasm."

"Good to know."

Sebastian turned his body so that it was parallel to the side of the wall were the ladder was. He laid down on the floor and eased his feet over the edge to look for the notches in the wall. Once he was sure he'd found them, he eased his way down the ladder a few feet and waved for Ciardis to follow when his head dipped below the ledge. "There will be a light orb trailing above me to light your path," he said, "but whatever you do, don't let go of the wall, okay?"

He continued his descent down into the hole and Ciardis quickly followed after. When she got to the bottom, he was standing there waiting. Turning left, he said, "Keep your hand on my shoulder at all times. The walls are spelled to induce hallucinations to uninvited guests."

"What a lovely place you've brought me to. I take it *you* are inviting me?"

He flashed her a sarcastic smile. "Yes, and the Land Wight should recognize my genuine desire for you to be here. If he doesn't, you'll probably be crushed alive."

"Ha ha, very funny," she grumbled.

"I wasn't joking that time."

She hastily placed a hand on his shoulder as they began to walk. Once beyond the sphere of light provided by the light orbs, they were encased in darkness, the light occasionally reflecting off the dampness of the tunnel walls. After a few minutes, Sebastian said in an oddly strained voice, "A portal way should soon appear – on our left side. We'll walk past that to a smooth stone wall. Above the smooth wall will be the Algardis crest, with a rearing lion carved into the stone."

Ciardis began looking to her left and then suddenly the portal way appeared like a mirage before her eyes. It glimmered in the wall in front of her, temptingly. The swirl of harnessed lightning and flickering color looked so inviting… She became entranced with the portal way, her escape from this tiny, claustrophobic tunnel.

Even with her hand on Sebastian's shoulder, Ciardis was beginning to have visions of dying in the depths of the mountain. *I could go anywhere,* she thought, taking a hesitant step forward. *I'd better leave now. The walls could cave in at any moment. I'd be trapped!* With that last thought, she dropped her hand from where it rested on Sebastian's shoulder and took a step toward the portal way.

Turning with a cry, Sebastian latched on to her hand tightly. "Don't listen to the portal way," he said harshly. "Concentrate! We're almost there. The portal way has desire spelled into it. It's fixating on your worst fears and making you experience them as if they're actually happening. If you step through that portal, I guarantee you that you'll find yourself in a far worse darkness than you're experiencing here."

She nodded, truly frightened for the first time, and he put her hand back on his shoulder. "We're almost there," he repeated.

Sebastian scanned the wall in front of him and said quietly, "There it is." He pointed toward the Algardis crest, carved into surface of the wall with deep lines. He reached for the stone carving. He gripped it firmly, obviously hoping that it recognized him as one of the Imperial line. It did. The gray wall rolled aside. Leading Ciardis through, Sebastian retrieved all his light orbs but two, expanding both of those until each was the size of a cart wheel.

Her eyes wide, Ciardis saw that they were now inside a vast cavern with carved walls, a roof supported by pillars, and a bridge that arched above a deep pit full of water. The way forward was wide enough for them to walk side by side. They crossed the bridge and headed straight for an elaborate doorway carved into the stone wall on the far side. Sebastian turned away from the door and knelt by a small stone urn near the edge of the bridge. He lifted it up and put it aside.

Then, with his fingertip, he traced a glyph into the small block set into the floor beneath the space the urn had occupied.

The glyph glowed golden for a moment; and then, with a faint *pop*, the block rose up from the floor. Smiling now, Sebastian reached down and pulled the block from its snug niche in the floor. He reached into the hole under it and brought up a lantern on a chain.

Ciardis said nothing but raised her eyebrows in speculation. Sebastian turned to her and asked sheepishly, "Um, do you have a match?"

"No."

"Tinderbox, by chance?"

"Of course not."

"Dreck. I forgot that I had to light the lantern," he said.

Ciardis sighed, shaking her head. Noting a few small flints lying on the ground, she bent down and, wincing at the destruction of the fine garment, tore a strip off of her tunic. She lifted her hand, "Give the lantern to me Sebastian. Please?"

After he handed over the lantern, she set it on the floor next to her, picked up a stone, and began to strike it against the wall, trying to catch a spark in the fabric. Luckily it was still bone dry, despite the dampness of the cavern, and she got the third spark going. Blowing on the baby flame, she nursed it until it was large enough to do the job, then managed to ignite the lantern's wick.

"Thanks," he said, grinning with relief. "I knew I brought you along for a reason."

As soon as the lantern was back in Sebastian's hands, the fire roared up between the glass panels and a bright light beamed straight from the wick to a small window far up on the ledge. They watched in wonder as the light reflected from that window to another, then another and another. Each responding glass window was set high in the wall. Soon, the glowing structure of a bridge made entirely of lantern light arced across the chamber, suspended in the air with no anchors.

Following Sebastian, Ciardis walked up and over the fire bridge to a ledge on the far side of the dark water. A second doorway lay beyond that ledge. This one was made of wood and had metal latches, and was much less elaborate than the first. Turning to her, Sebastian asked, "May I borrow your knife?"

She flipped the blade out of her belt and handed it over. He cut a tiny slice into the palm of his hand and pressed his torn skin to the door. "The final door requires a blood sacrifice," he explained.

They heard a lock click, and several bars slid back into the doorframe. Then it swung open. The room beyond was filled with light and five very large, very angry lions. Ciardis blanched and immediately began to back up.

"No," whispered Sebastian urgently, "follow my lead. Always."

Ciardis stopped backing up, but she stayed behind Sebastian. If anyone was going to get eaten, it was going to be him.

Raising his hand, Sebastian showed his bloody palm to each lion. Ciardis didn't think that was such a good idea, but kept her mouth shut. To her astonishment, each of the five lion took a whiff, backed away, and lay down on its stomach.

Calmly, she and Sebastian walked through the seated pride and into the next chamber. She sighed in relief as soon as the lions were far behind them. "How long is this going to take?" she asked in a low voice.

"As long as it takes," replied Sebastian.

She resisted the urge to whack him on the back of his head. He was, after all, the Prince Heir.

Once again they were walking through a tunnel; this one wound about a bit more, however, and offered more room to maneuver. She wasn't sure how much later in their journey it was when Sebastian stopped at a raised platform in the center of the corridor. It was unremarkable: a solid block of plain, square stone that rose up four or five feet from the ground. He hauled himself up onto the platform, then reached down to grip Ciardis's wrist and help her scramble up the side.

Moving to the center of the platform, he waited. With a creak and a groan, the stone cube they were standing upon began to levitate. It moved straight upward, and Ciardis quickly looked up, expecting to see a stone ceiling ready to squash them. But the ceiling, which had been there only a few seconds before, had disappeared and been replaced by nothing but darkness. The ride was a bit jerky, and each of them wrapped their hands around the other's waist for balance.

When the stone platform finished rising and clicked into place, they stood in a large, cavernous room with a smooth stone floor, rounded walls, and a quiet ambience. As they stepped off the platform, a multicolored light began to pulse in mid-air. It flickered between many forms: a tree, a bird in flight, a grassy knoll, a mountain stream. It never stayed in one form for very long. Most disconcertingly, it wept. Drops of water condensed on the rocks and fell down in eerie drips, thunderous rain wracked the grassy knoll, and thin rills poured down the trunk of the tree.

It was the Land Wight, and it was clearly in severe pain.

Horrified, but determined to do something, Ciardis walked up to the elemental and laid her hand on its side. Underneath the skin, the fur, the bark, the grass— a rhythmic thud sounded – like the heartbeat of a living thing, and a creature that gasped and sobbed in sorrow.

She closed her eyes in empathy. "Don't you feel it?" she whispered to Sebastian, her head resting on the shuddering and shifting skin, fur, bark, grass, leaves. He stood by her side, close to but not touching the Land Wight.

When it shuddered again, Ciardis reached for Sebastian's hand automatically. Without even thinking, she drew him forward into its embrace. The Land Wight had stopped shifting for the moment; it was a full-grown maple tree now. Sap leaked from cracks in its bark like the tears of a weeping woman.

Ciardis extended her entire body to embrace the tree. Without saying a word, she urged Sebastian to do the same.

The Prince Heir opened his arms wide and pushed his body into the bark.

From the moment he'd entered the room, he'd had no idea what to do. Oh, he'd felt the Wight's pain on some level for years, but it had never been like this before. He'd supplied the codes without fail, providing the blood required, and, most of all, he'd followed protocol.

Hugging a powerful elemental wasn't in protocol. But Ciardis, an untrained mage, had known instinctively what to do. He had no doubt now that they were meant to be here together—perhaps even to go through life together.

Sebastian bit back a cry as he dropped the mental barriers on his mind, opening his magic to the Land Wight. He needed to know what it felt, what it saw, to cause such intensity of emotion. As he threw the gates to his soul wide, the elemental's images of the life and energy that powered Algardis came pouring in. It couldn't talk—not in the form it was in now—but it could show them and help them experience what it felt.

They saw and felt the iciness of winter on the Northern border. More disconcertingly, they felt the thrum of many boots crossing the perilous lands. The boots marched in concert with many heartbeats. They were soldiers—foreigners—on its soil.

The Land Wight showed them how it fought the foreigners to the best of its ability. It conjured snowstorms, ice, and hail to make the soldiers' march difficult. It made the land inhospitable to the foreign troops with the death of crops and a dearth of sunshine. But it was a taxing effort, one it was trying its best to maintain, but could not for much longer…not without help.

They experienced its fear—no, its *frustration*—at its near-helplessness. The absence of the Algardis blood fighting by its side was conspicuous in its mind.

The pain that was wracking it arose from the constant pressure of maintaining such an intense assault on the invading troops without its traditional partner.

Having learned all that he needed to, Sebastian hesitantly reached out to the Land Wight's presence. Through its pain, he sent waves of comfort and reassurance to it. He indicated as best he could that he and Ciardis needed to step back for a moment, but that they were there to help, to put an end to its pain.

Mentally sighing with acceptance, it allowed them to withdraw from its visions, to pull back into their own minds and untangle their physical forms from its bark. Gratefully, Sebastian stepped back, pulling Ciardis back, as well. When he had caught his breath again, he said to her, "Do you know how dangerous that was?"

"It needed our help."

"It needs more than just *our* help. Remember when I mentioned that each person within the Algardis court is connected to the land, or should be?"

She nodded. As he tiredly ran his fingers through his hair, he said, "Apparently those bonds used to be much stronger. They were even strong enough for the Land Wight or the Emperor to draw upon in times of peril."

"Alright. So?"

"So what's going on? Why isn't my father helping the Land Wight guard against the hordes gathering in the North? Where's the connection between the Court and the land?" Sebastian looked with sadness at the forlorn tree in the middle of the chamber. Softly, he said, "Why does it stand there with no aid?"

The tree shuddered. Twisting its branches, it snapped them in anger at Ciardis and Sebastian. "It wants us to come back," she said softly.

Sebastian put a warning hand on her arm. "Stronger mages have died in the Land Wight's embrace, Ciardis."

"Well then, we'll just have to make sure it knows we're here to help."

"That's not what I meant," he muttered as he watched her approach the trembling tree once more. *She treats it like a pet, but that tree is one of the greatest forces of nature this world has ever seen.*

Shuddering, he stepped forward again. They gripped the bark with their arms, their legs, and their bodies, and turned their faces into its embrace. "Here we are," Ciardis cooed softly to the tree.

It began to send them images again, but this time, the images took the form of answers to their concerns. The first images that came were of Sebastian's grandfather and his great-grandfather kneeling before the elemental in obeisance, asking for its guidance and its embrace. Then they saw the same men as infants, with proud Imperial parents hovering over them at their christenings. The Land Wight stood to one side of the crowd of courtiers, invisible but present. The only people who seemed to notice the unseen elemental were the children in their cradles, who tried to grasp its airy substance, and their fathers—the Emperors—who smiled in secret pride at the vision of the elemental that they and their children shared.

During the christenings, the Land Wight gave its blessings and benedictions to each child, welcoming them gently into its fold.

But conspicuously absent was the benediction of Sebastian's father and then his father's obeisance during his teenage years. *Where is he?* Sebastian asked the Land Wight. It answered with a void of darkness, a blank emptiness. It had never embraced the latest Algardis Emperor, never provided its benison, and that was when the Empire had begun to fold.

But why?

The Land Wight answered Ciardis's query to the best of its ability, showing them more images of the boy who was now a man, the prince who was now the emperor, *the ruler who was not a mage.* Sebastian shuddered in horror. *The Land Wight is saying that my father has no magic, no bond, and no power!*

"How could this happen?" he whispered to himself as he withdrew. "The Imperial court would have known, *should have known,* if their emperor wasn't a mage. He had to go through multiple initiation ceremonies including the offering, the obeisance, and the soul bonds."

"How?" said Ciardis. "How would they have known? You've kept the Land Wight's location secret. No one knows it's here."

"Yes, but the connection of the Court to the land cannot be faked! The Emperor is that connection from the courts to the land; the Land Wight is the conduit from the land to the Emperor," Sebastian said angrily. "There are ceremonies my father has had to perform every year since he was a child. He's gone through them – I've seen them. The very same ceremonies that I have gone through myself!"

He left unsaid the fact that he had failed in those ceremonies.

Denial came roaring through into Sebastian's mind. The Land Wight was saying as clear as day that he was wrong – that the emperor had *not* performed the ceremonies. After a few tense seconds, the message became clearer: the Land Wight had taken on the duty of renewing the Courts connection to the lands – weakening itself in the process.

Sebastian relayed this to Ciardis and she tried to process all that they had learned.

"Semantics," Sebastian said tiredly.

"I don't think so," Ciardis said with excitement. "What if the Land Wight has been maintaining the connection this whole time?"

Sebastian was ready to object that that was impossible. Then, abruptly, the Land Wight began to send another flood of images their way. This time, it was too confusing to understand. "Whoa, whoa," said Sebastian. "Slow down—*please.* We don't understand. We can't understand."

The images lessened in intensity as the Land Wight drew back. It began to form a slideshow of their mental images. The projected images showed them that the Land Wight hadn't wanted the land to suffer even if the Emperor didn't—or couldn't—hear its needs. In order to make sure the land's needs were met, the Land Wight had gone to every ceremony from the annual Blessing of the Court to the Midsummer's Bloodletting for the fall harvest. Each time, it had poured from its own reserves the measure of geological magic required to activate the spell bonding the land and the Algardis family.

The land magic had come from it, but should have been coming from the Emperor. And then it got worse.

Sebastian was born, and the Land Wight rejoiced. Here was its partner and conduit to the Court, the one who would help it strengthen the crops and protect the people. It was clear from the early days of his life that Sebastian had the power necessary to partner with the land and join in union with the Land Wight.

Ciardis and Sebastian saw an image of the Land Wight hovering over Sebastian as a baby, its emotions dominated by joy. They saw the waves of power that rose from Sebastian's cradle even as a child. They felt the Land Wight's anticipation. It had been waiting until the first obeisance ceremony, when Sebastian turned five, to introduce itself and initiate the bond between the Prince Heir and the land.

But that never happened.

The Land Wight showed them a horrible place with dead trees, rotten fruits, and terrible odors. Its own version of a living nightmare. The night before Sebastian turned five a man had come into his room. He had not meant the boy physical harm, so the Land Wight had no ability to fight him. He had come and he had formed a spell as the Land Wight watched in grief.

The spell drew power from Sebastian's mage core, draining it little by little in a continuous spiral into a small locket. After the spell was done, a golden thread rose from the core of the child's magic and connected to the locket.

The Land Wight showed the locket being presented to the Emperor as a gift, and then it showed the sudden manifestation of the Emperor's power. But the new, unlocked power wasn't the Emperor's.

It was all from Sebastian—drained from his mage core every hour of every day.

The Land Wight watched in grief, but could do nothing. What was worse was that the locket gave the Emperor the power to act as a guardian of the land, but never gave him the insight to connect with the Land Wight itself—the insight that every Algardis Emperor was born and died with, the ability to feel a disturbance in a distance mountain pass or unease passing through a forest as darkness wafted through.

"He didn't have it. My father didn't have the insight born to the Emperors," said Sebastian in shock. He stumbled back and sat on the ground in confusion.

He sat and thought about what the Land Wight had shown them for a few moments. Then he denied it, "My father couldn't have known."

Ciardis crouched in front of him, placing her hands on his arms.

"There has to be an explanation," he said.

"I'm sure there is."

"How could my father accept the gift? How could he not know it was coming from me? Stolen from me. Didn't he notice something was wrong?"

"I'm sure he would have done something if he had known. Non-mages can't sense magic. He probably never even suspected you'd been drained if you looked whole and healthy. He must have thought his sudden surge of ability was a gift from the Gods."

Getting up, Sebastian flung a hand angrily at the Land Wight. "Do you think it can tell us who did this and why?"

"I think the Land Wight has shown us as much as it can. It has been helping your family for generations. It didn't give up on you; you shouldn't give up on it."

"Right," said Sebastian.

Hesitantly placing his hand on the Land Wight's trunk, he showed it his sorrow, and his gratitude for its continued care of the land. *How do I take my place as your partner?*

It gave him a warning flash of power, and then opened its mind. Sebastian fell into it, and Ciardis hurried to grab the prince's suddenly falling body. Cradling his body she eased them down until they sat on the floor – his body in her arms. Grabbing his hand she pressed it to the Land Wight's trunk. She desperately hoped Sebastian was still breathing.

He was, but his breaths were shallow.

Sebastian? Sebastian! She called out desperately, mind-to-mind.

From far away, she heard his thoughts whisper, *I'm here. But it's too much.* There was pain laced through his voice. *Too much power from the Land Wight all at once, and not enough from me,* he said. *I'll lose all ties to my magic if I can't break that locket's connection.*

"Then let's break it!" Ciardis said aloud.

As one, they dove down towards his mage core, searching with their second sight for the golden thread that linked his magic to the locket. It wasn't hard to find. It lay like a fine, pale line lancing out from his core and going straight into the Aether, off into the darkness straight towards the locket nestled at the Algardis Emperor's throat.

They stared at the pulsing thread, which beat in time with the Prince's heart. Neither could see a weakness, a strand out of place, or a thin spot where it might be broken. Brushing her mind with his,

Sebastian said, *I think I can do it. I can see where it connects to my core. I can cut it off from there—but I need your help.*

She nodded from where she sat beside the Land Wight before she realized he couldn't see that in his unconscious state, and then said simply, "You have it."

He went to work, first locking down and turning off his mage core, then gripping the thread that lanced it as best he could. It felt like holding his breath for far too long, but as long as his mage core was locked down, the thread couldn't draw upon the core to strengthen itself. It began to weaken, and he kept insistently tugging on it. Inch by inch, it withdrew from the core of his magic like a parasitic water worm being withdrawn from a swollen sore. Like a spool of thread winding down, the parasitic thread came out of his mage core piece by piece until he had the very tip in his grip, and with a sharp tug, he snapped it. Ciardis could feel the *snap* resound through her body as Sebastian drew upon her power for the final act, and her soul sang out with joy.

As soon as it snapped, his power came rushing in. The power had dwindled to a pitiful ghost now blazed with the power of a contained sun. Ciardis hurried to pull her mind back from his. Even looking at Sebastian's mage core for too long was blinding.

Just before she reached her own mind, she felt the Land Wight and Sebastian meet as equals at last. The Land Wight began raining leaves down upon Sebastian's still form and Ciardis's smiling face.

It had been waiting fifteen years to feel that bond again—the bond of an Algardis Emperor to the land.

CHAPTER SEVENTEEN

Moments later, Sebastian awoke in her arms. "How does it feel?" she asked him.

He gave her a tired but elated smile. "Amazing."

She smiled back at him. He sat up, feeling a little dizzy for a few moments, but fine overall. Meanwhile, the Land Wight towered over them in its tree form, leaves and flowers blossoming on its limbs as if it were the peak of spring.

"Well, it looks like *someone* is happy," Ciardis said with a soft smile.

Sebastian laughed before he said, "It is—I can feel it. Already its power grows. Right now I'm just bolstering it, but soon I should be able to monitor certain land activities myself, leaving the Land Wight free to guard the realm."

"All right, then." Ciardis got up and dusted herself off, then leaned forward to put her hand on the Land Wight's trunk. It immediately sent her its joy…and thanks. She sent back waves of satisfaction in return. Turning to Sebastian, she said, "I think it's time we left."

Nodding, he turned and said his own private goodbye to the Land Wight.

As she started walking back toward the platform, Sebastian called out, "Wait. There's an exit from the mountain in this room." Sebastian indicated the far wall with a tilt of his head. "There's a portal down the passageway that will take us out, back to the mortal realm. We've been here far too long anyway."

"Right," Ciardis said, stifling a yawn. "I have no idea what I'll tell my sponsor when I get back."

Sebastian shrugged. "The truth might not hurt. Just say you were with one of your patron candidates."

Ciardis let out an undignified snort. "Right! I guess I can do that."

Grinning, he threw an arm around her shoulders and they proceeded to exit the chamber side-by-side, the tree blossoming behind them; alone again, but not forgotten.

They walked up a tunnel with a steep incline, and soon they saw the portal way up ahead. It was literally built to span the tunnel, like a pool of shimmering light, and was the only way out. Ciardis asked, "You *do* know where this will take us, right?"

"It should take us right back to where we started in the maze," he said. "Your anklet will direct it."

They walked forward, and this time she didn't feel the stomach-twisting tug of magic, but rather a swirl of power—almost as if they were in a magical whirlpool.

When they arrived, the first thing Ciardis noticed was that they were *not* in the maze.

They stood in a room before a group of people that Ciardis was quite unfamiliar with—that is, if she didn't count her ticked-off sponsor and tutorials instructor standing in the huddle of nobility. After glancing at Serena and Damias, Ciardis couldn't help but gawk at the other fifteen or so people who crowded the room, all of who wore the finest court dress.

A man cleared his throat; he wore the badge of the Gardis and had an imposing stature, and he stood at attention before Sebastian. His dark brown eyes didn't twitch, and not a muscle moved on his dark skin as he calmly announced, "The Prince has returned. All Hail Prince Sebastian Athanos Algardis."

"All Hail," came the quiet murmur from the surrounding courtiers. Stepping forward, he clasped Sebastian's hand in his own as he leaned toward him and whispered, "It's good to see you alive, my Prince. When even your mind link disappeared, we feared the worst."

Sebastian nodded sharply. "Yes, I should have thought of that. I hope Allora wasn't too concerned, Commander."

The commander said nothing, merely stepped back with a bow and turned to face north once more.

With a groan, Ciardis met the eyes of Patricia, whose gloating could not be ignored. *You're in trouble now,* came the telepathic taunt, laced with vindictive amusement.

Ciardis, covered in dirt and tired as all hell, pulled back her lips in what could charitably be called a smile, but most would read as the bared teeth of an animal ready to bite.

Ciardis noticed Patricia's perfectly coiffed hair and beautiful rose-colored gown, wondering, *'Why is she wearing her second day outfit? It shouldn't be worn until tomorrow's Hunt.'*

And then she looked around at the lords and ladies gathered, embarrassed at her abrupt entrance, not to mention her disheveled appearance.

What must they think of me? Out all night…with a patron.

But they weren't staring at her; no, they were all staring *through* Ciardis and Sebastian with the looks of disdain that the nobility usually reserved for those special moments whenever they stepped in horse droppings.

Self-consciously, Ciardis looked down at herself. She knew she was covered in dust and dirt, and her hair must be a tangled mess. But that didn't quite explain their stone-cold reception.

Finally, Serena looked her dead in the eye, gave her an icy glare and the hand signal to bow deeply.

Ciardis hesitantly did what she asked, and a harsh whisper echoed from one of the gathered nobles. "Turn around, you fools."

Ciardis looked to Sebastian, who had turned pale. *Interesting—he looks like he swallowed a grape and it went down the wrong way.* He was that gray. Together, they mentally decided to do as commanded and turned their backs to the crowd, hoping not to get shot in the back with an irritated bolt of lightning from a highly-strung duke standing in the back corner.

As soon as she did, she saw the reason her sponsor was furious, and the reason she was never going to live this down.

A haughty man stood in front of them wearing resplendent court robes, an aloof expression, and the crown of an emperor.

Ciardis fell to her knees and huddled on the floor, wishing it would swallow her up—or, at the very least, that her dirty hair would untwist from the tangle of braids and hide her flaming face. Sebastian wasn't so servile, but he did swiftly drop to one knee.

"My son, welcome back to Court," the Emperor said upon turning his gaze to the Prince Heir.

"Thank you, Father," Sebastian said as he stood pulling Ciardis up with him by her elbow. Ciardis was fairly sure she heard an audible gasp from Serena's direction. She didn't dare look; she would *never* live this down.

She also resented Sebastian's insistence that she stand up. She'd rather have stayed right where she was, huddled on the floor and close to being out of sight.

"Father," said Sebastian, apparently reluctant to speak in front of the Court. "May we speak privately?"

"I'm certain, Lord Sebastian, that your disdain for protocol, blatant dereliction of duty, and complete failure to inform the Gardis of your whereabouts—requiring the use of quite a bit of mage power to redirect your Aether bracelet—can be discussed publicly," interrupted his father's Grand Vizier.

Sebastian looked to his father to slap the vizier down for his impertinence, but the Emperor merely steeped his fingers and waited. Sebastian frowned and prepared to make his case before his father and the court.

As Ciardis looked over at the vizier she realized something shocking. She needed to talk to Sebastian mind-to-mind *now*. But she couldn't project her thoughts without touching, only receive them. As he opened his mouth to speak, Ciardis grabbed his hand and gripped it hard. She stood close enough to him that their cloaks hid the movement from the courtiers gathered behind them but not, of course, his father in front of them.

She hoped she imagined the faint look of surprise on the Emperor's face.

What? He snapped through their connection.

She ignored his rudeness and the snide look from the Grand Vizier, who was waiting for Sebastian to make his case, and sent to Sebastian, *That's the man from the vision—the one who created that stupid locket in the first place!*

Sebastian's face didn't betray his thoughts as he carefully recalled the vision, looking over the scene of the strange man standing over his bed just before he turned five and thought over Ciardis's claim. *Damn it, you're right.* He couldn't deny it.

Turning to the Grand Vizier, he said, "There's certainly much we could discuss, my Lord Vizier, but my primary concern is why you have been siphoning off my mage powers for so long."

The gathered courtiers gasped, though his lord father remained conspicuously silent. Ciardis snuck a peek at the Emperor through lowered eyes and saw that he looked perplexed. "Explain yourself, Sebastian," his father commanded after a long moment.

Sebastian called golden fire to his palms. "This, Father, is what I mean," said Sebastian slowly. "I haven't been able to call the healing fire from the land since I was a toddler. I can now do this and more. I visited our Land Wight tonight. I saw what the Grand Vizier had done – he's been stealing my mage powers for a decade."

"Lies, Sire," shouted the Grand Vizier as he hurried forth to prostrate himself before the Emperor, much to Sebastian's disgust. "I would never do anything to harm the Imperial Throne!" he babbled, rising to his knees with a panicked look in his eyes.

The Emperor stepped forward and caught the Vizier's chin in his grip.

"If what my son says is true, Vizier, there is *nothing* that would excuse it."

"I can *explain,* Sire—" But before the Vizier could finish the thought, his voice was cut off, as if a vise had clasped itself around his throat. The man tumbled back to the floor, gasping for air and clawing at his throat desperately.

As people surged forward to help, he clawed at his own throat in a desperate attempt to gain air. He was clearly fighting for breath that would not come. His eyes began to bulge, and he silently pleaded for help as blood vessels burst on the edges on his corneas. He fell back suddenly, and then lay very still.

The Grand Vizier was dead.

The Emperor ordered in the Gardis and had the room sealed.

Summoning the Commander of the Imperial Guard, the Emperor quickly ordered a mental inspection of all the room's inhabitants. Four of the Gardis went from person to person, looking for the murderer who had to be a mage of strong Air Magic, who had sufficient skills to take the breath from a person's lungs. It was a rare level of magic not easily attained, with only a few known practitioners able to do it, two of which resided as Instructors at the Red Madrassa.

After questioning everyone from the lowest non-mage courtier to Sebastian himself, it was determined that none had the ability to do what had been done to the Vizier. The killer wasn't in the room.

Tersely, the Emperor ordered the Commander of the Imperial Guard and Sebastian to join him in an antechamber. Sebastian kept a firm grip on Ciardis's hand. Tugging her behind him even though she would have much preferred to be in a different room from the irate Emperor. With tenseness in his stride that telegraphed his anger, the Emperor asked, "How? *How*, Sebastian, was your magic stolen?"

Sebastian paled; he wasn't ready to accuse his father of betrayal, wasn't yet ready to hear him admit to the crime.

"Sebastian," said the Emperor sharply.

The Prince Heir sighed and took a deep breath. "Through a locket, Father. The gold one you wear about your neck."

Reaching inside his robes, the Emperor pulled out the simple gold chain and oval locket. He pulled it off and handed it to the commander with a simple, "Test it."

"Aye, Sire."

Sebastian swallowed hard. His father's face was expressionless, neither disbelieving nor angered. They waited in tense silence while the commander tested the necklace and returned it to the Emperor's hands after a brief inspection. "It's as the young prince says, Sire. It has residual ties leading even now to his mage core."

"Break the ties, then," the Emperor said.

"They're already dissipating on their own, Father." Sebastian stood facing him, waiting for some sign—*any* sign—that he hadn't known.

Finally, the Emperor wiped a tired hand on his face. "I don't know how this came to be, Sebastian. The mage power within the locket—yes, I knew that some power was there—was intended for use only as a reserve. I have never had to consciously call upon it, and I certainly never knew that it was tied to you."

A shudder went through the Emperor at that moment, and he dropped to his knees with a quick gasp of pain. The commander was by his side in moments, carefully tending to the ruler.

Sebastian knelt by his father's side, clutching his hand. By then, the Emperor had collapsed entirely.

"There's much you don't know, son," the Emperor said with a brittle laugh. "But for now, I don't have time to explain." Another shudder wracked his body. "You and...your friend...have freed up...the power of the Land Wight, which I should have had the courage to do myself...years ago," the Emperor stated. "Now that it is done, the power is surging through the land and breaking the...pacts I've had in place with the others."

"*Others?*" said Sebastian sharply.

"That is not for your knowledge," said his father, catching his breath at last and struggling to his feet. "Not yet. I must deal with this immediately. You have regained your birthright and everything pertaining thereunto. You have my congratulations. Attend to the festivities, and we will discuss your duties at a later point," the Emperor commanded.

Sebastian felt frustration and ire flash through him. He wanted to know *now*; he didn't care to be turned away. But he had no choice. He bowed stiffly and was escorted out. Ciardis following in his wake. Once back in the main salon, Sebastian motioned for the other nobles to leave the room and went with the Master of Ceremonies to ensure that the grounds were cleared of all potential threats.

Never once did he look back at Ciardis.

 194

CHAPTER EIGHTTEEN

The carriage was silent as they passed through city in the early dawn. After some time had passed, Lady Serena looked at Ciardis and asked, "Do you know what time it is?"

"Close to dawn, milady," said Ciardis, her heart pounding in her chest.

"And do you know what *day* it is?"

"The second day of the Patron Hunt."

"Really?" said Serena with a soft laugh.

Damias interrupted their terse conversation with an irritated cough. "Ciardis, you were missing for a full day and night. Your second day has come and gone. All your Patrons have rescinded their invitations. We were at court to declare you a missing person and have the Gardis conduct a search."

"Ha! Do you know what fools we looked like?" exclaimed Serena. "We went before the Emperor begging for his help, and there you appeared, covered in dust and dirt, with not a scratch on you!"

Even Damias regarded her in disappointment.

Then Serena lost it. "How could you do this to us, you ungrateful wretch?"

Damias winced, but said nothing.

"I...I didn't know. The prince needed my help, and I couldn't refuse," she whispered, bowing her head.

"The prince needed your *help*?" Serena said cruelly. "He needs everyone's help—the brat is useless! Did he not tell you that his father has issued orders for him to abdicate his place in the succession?"

"Well, no, but—"

"Ah, so he *also* didn't tell you that this abdication will take place tomorrow," said Serena. "Whatever he promised you—wealth, titles, land—he has *no* claim to it. You gave up a place as the premier companion Trainee and a place within the Companions' Guild for nothing."

"Serena, I never intended to take anything from him. He has asked for nothing—" And then Ciardis stopped suddenly, finally understanding Serena's words. "Given up?" she said. This time, Damias would not look at her at all, instead staring out the window with single-minded intensity.

"Your contract as a trainee with the Companions' Guild has been terminated, effective immediately," said Serena.

Ciardis gasped in horror.

"Serena, please," begged Ciardis, all pretense gone. "I...I...General Barnaren has indicated his interest, and so has Viscount Marce. They are both credits to the Companions' Guild!"

"They are not enough," snapped Serena. "As I've said before, your other Patron candidates have withdrawn. Now show *some* dignity."

At that moment, the carriage stopped and Serena leapt out. As she walked away, she said over her shoulder, "Your things are packed. You'll be on your way to Vaneis within the hour."

As Ciardis turned to look for Damias she saw he was already out the other door. "Coward!" she shouted, furious. She sat down heavily on the carriage steps, her mind filled with anger.

"Hey, lass," called the driver. "We have to move. Off with you."

She stood up and moved away from the conveyance. With a flick of his whip, the driver urged the horses towards the barn.

In a daze, she made her way back to her room, where—true to Serena's word—three trunks sat in the middle of the room, packed and ready to go.

Kneeling in front of one, she opened it and gazed at all the court dresses bought for her by the Companions' Guild and the books she'd collected over her months in Sandrin. Sighing, she stood up and dusted off her hands. She eyed the dirt caked on her palms with disgust. *I might as well take one last shower.*

After unpacking a simple tunic and trousers, she went and did just that. Towards the end, hot water running down her back and soap in her hair—which had taken forever to unbraid—she luxuriated in the soothing hot water for the last time. Then, rinsing off and grabbing a towel, she prepared to step out of the shower. She felt around on the side of the tub for her towel, which was supposed to be hanging on the wall hook.

"Here," said a voice, and someone handed her the towel. Ciardis bit back a scream, snatching the towel in a rush to cover her nakedness. When she finally placed the voice, she screamed, "How *dare* you! This is my private bathing area, Sebastian! What the hell are you doing in here?"

"If you could stop screaming for just a second—"

"You certainly left me without as much as a word earlier—"

"Ciardis, really…"

"Get out!"

"I can't."

"Why? Do you need my *help* again?" she sneered, stepping out of the tub to grab a second towel for her hair.

"Don't say it like that."

"Like what?"

"Like you're somehow worthless," he snapped.

"Well, let's see," she said, moving around the bathroom. "My patrons have abandoned me, my prince *lied* to me, I've been kicked out of the Companion' Guild—oh, and a person I *thought* was a friend left me in the Emperor's audience room without so much as a goodbye."

Sebastian turned around and around, following her as she paced in a circle. "I didn't abandon you, I *am* your friend, and I never lied to you," he protested.

"Oh no?" she scoffed. "My sources say otherwise. You also neglected to mention that you're about to be disinherited!"

"I *was* about to be disinherited, but that was contingent upon my not regaining my powers. Thanks to you, I have my powers back in full."

"Right," she said, stopping suddenly. "So—you owe me?"

"Right. Wait…what?"

"You. Owe. Me."

"I might agree to *help* you," he said haughtily.

"You stubborn bastard! Let's cut the shit. I'm being kicked out of the Companions' Guild. I need you to do something about that. Without me, you wouldn't have been able to break the locket's embrace *or* connect it to the Grand Vizier."

Sebastian looked at her with a face eerily similar to his father's: aloof and cold, though much younger. "Fine," he said softly. "Consider it done."

Within the hour, her candidacy was reinstated, invitations were received to dine with Princess Heir Marissa of Sandrin *and* Initiate Soundsoar of the Madrassa that night, an ambitious General was already making his rounds in the Companions' Guild, and all of it was done with the conspicuous absence of Viscount Iskas of Marce.

After hours of insipid conversation with Damias—who had the grace to at least *look* ashamed about abandoning her—and Serena—who acted like nothing more untoward had happened than a misplaced hairpin—Ciardis decided to prepare herself for the night's dinner.

The Princess Heir and Initiate Soundsoar had agreed to host the dinner together, leaving Ciardis intrigued. She knew of no companion with more than one Patron, but there was a first time for everything.

The invitation had been specific: she was to come in loose but comely attire. She chose a short but airy dress with cap sleeves, room for a small back sheath, and sandals that laced up her calves. The light blue color complimented her dusky skin well, and the moonstone and sapphire Aether bracelet flashed on her ankle. She had yet to take it off.

Night had already fallen when they arrived at the Princess Heir's palace. Ciardis and Damias descended from the carriage. A chamberlain hurried forward a moment later to show them to the dining suite.

A long, low table was laden with foods and wine of every variety. At the head of the table sat a beautiful woman with a riot of black, curly hair and skin the color of walnuts. She wore gold bangles on her wrist and her neck, while her face was beautifully made up.

"She's stunning," Ciardis whispered to Damias as they walked toward where the woman sat.

He surveyed their hostess with a critical eye before muttering, "She's on the market."

Ciardis laughed. "So am I. What does that make the pair of us?"

"Two beautiful women who could take the Summer Imperial

dances by storm," interjected a man with a booming voice.

Ciardis gasped in surprise and Damias grinned, turning to greet the man walking toward them. The voice belonged to the same man she'd met in the Imperial gardens ages ago – Lord Aaron.

"Soundsoar," he exclaimed. "It's been too long."

"You haven't changed, Damias," he said, and they gripped hands in the odd way that men do.

"Ciardis Weathervane, may I present Lord Soundsoar?" Damias said with a grand bow.

Soundsoar looked at her and winked. Ciardis blushed, "It's an honor to meet you, milord."

"And you, as well, my dear. I hear that you have *quite* the interesting tale to tell."

Ciardis nodded politely in acknowledgement and Soundsoar gestured to the head of the table, where Princess Heir Marissa awaited them casually.

Ciardis walked to the head of the table to greet the woman. She heard Damias say behind her, "After you, milord."

As she approached the reclining princess, Ciardis dipped into a gentle curtsy. "Milady, it pleases me to make your acquaintance."

The princess sat up languidly and then stood. With the subtle movement of a snake, she circled around Ciardis, looking her over from head to toe. Finally, she met her eyes.

"Well, well, the rumors are true...a beautiful Weathervane has once again come to grace the Court of Sandrin."

"At your service, Your Imperial Highness."

A bright laugh like glass shards falling on a polished floor escaped from the princess's mouth. Ciardis felt a bit of uneasy – the Princess Heir's voice was familiar to her too. But she couldn't place from where.

"You certainly shall be."

Turning abruptly, she called for her retainers. Servants poured into the room from hidden doors, holding trays laden with soups, salads, appetizers, and cakes. The table soon groaned under the weight of the additional food.

She raised a glass in a toast to a successful evening.

Hours later, dazed but proud with her successful evening with the Princess Heir and Lord Soundsoar, Ciardis asked, "Milady, I beg that you appease my curiosity. You are princess heir to which province, if I might ask? It's one of the fascinating subjects not covered in my dossiers."

Ciardis was a little tipsy, or she would have noticed the flash of anger in the woman's eyes.

With a smile masking her ire, the Princess Heir raised her glass of wine. "Why, the whole of the Algardis Empire, my dear."

Ciardis glanced over at Damias in confusion. He looked just as uncertain. She turned back to the Princess Heir just in time to see a flash of mage power out of the corner of her eye.

I thought those damn mage sight flashes were supposed to go away?

Then she felt the bind of bands of air across her throat. She couldn't breathe.

And then she knew no more.

CHAPTER NINETEEN

When Ciardis awoke, she lay in a small dark, bedroom on a pallet on the floor. Wincing, she realized that her throat was sore from whatever the Air Mage had done to her. As she looked around the room she saw Damias lying in a heap next to the far wall.

She quickly got up and went over to his sprawled form, afraid of what she might find. She shook his shoulder and looked for any indication that he was breathing, and she sighed in relief when he groaned and opened his eyes.

"Careful, careful," she said as she helped him sit up. From the dark and colorful bruises around his neck, it looked like he had borne the brunt of the attack.

"Ciardis, where are we?"

"I don't know—some room. I just woke up."

"This is Soundsoar's doing."

"But how? And why?"

"He's an Air Mage—he holds a position at the Madrassa. I remember the Gardis questioning me about the death of the Grand

Vizier. They said an Air Mage of incomparable power assassinated him."

"Sounds like he was responsible, then." She hesitated. "Why didn't you bring that up in the Emperor's chambers?"

Damias said ruefully, "I didn't know he was in town."

Deciding it was best to tell him, Ciardis said, "I met him once. But I didn't know it was him!"

Damias peered her intently, "What?"

"I went to the Imperial Gardens and he was there. He introduced himself as Lord Aaron and we barely spent a few minutes together."

Damias sighed. "It's not your fault. This is on Soundsoar. Honestly, I thought he was of better character than that. Goes to show you don't know your friends."

"No, you don't," said Soundsoar from the open door.

Both Ciardis and Damias scrambled to their feet to face him.

Damias stepped forward. "What's this about?"

"The Imperial Throne," replied Soundsoar. "What else?"

"We have nothing to do with that," Ciardis said from Damias's side.

"On the contrary my dear, *you* have everything to do with it," replied Soundsoar. "If you hadn't butted your silly head in, the prince would have been disavowed today, packed off to some small town by nightfall, and Her Imperial Highness would be sitting for crown measurements this evening."

"Now we have to kill the emperor," Soundsoar said with some regret.

"What?" said Ciardis. "Sebastian is the rightful heir—all I did was restore his power."

"Precisely," came the irate hiss of the woman standing behind Soundsoar. "I've drained Sebastian since childhood. Painstakingly renewing the necklace's spell and even planting it on the Emperor to ensure I wasn't linked to the crime if it was discovered. I've waited for the day when Sebastian would fail the final test. You have undone ten years of preparation and patience. For that, I'll have your life."

The princess continued as if by afterthought, "And your power."

Soundsoar ordered the guards to come in and drag the two captives from the room. Damias and Ciardis were forced out of the palace and towards one of the prison towers of Sandrin. Built like a needle, the tower pointed straight up into the sky.

The princess ranted nonstop the whole way.

"I proved time and again to my father, Emperor Cymus – who was Sebastian's grandfather - my worth, my strength, my skills as a leader," she began.

Ciardis's wrists were bound behind her back. She began struggling silently with the ties.

"I wanted him to declare me Heir Presumptive. But he did nothing but quote history to me: *The firstborn male must take the throne.*"

"*I* am the first born, *I* should have taken the throne," she said disgust in her voice.

Ciardis caught Damias's eye as they continued walking up the winding tower steps. He shook his head—whether to tell her not to try anything or that the Princess Heir was crazy, she didn't know.

They kept rising. Ciardis had counted over a hundred steps so far.

"I begged him. Then my father made me Princess Heir in the event of the death of my brother, the current Emperor. But he had a condition – I could only ascend the throne if my brother died with no legitimate heir who could tie to the land. I had what I needed. I killed my father with a slow poison. I was *supposed* to take the throne after that insipid brother of mine died off, but no—suddenly that brat, my nephew, was born, and all my waiting was for naught," said the princess, anger rising in her tone.

They finally reached the eye of the needle. The room was empty except shackles on the wall.

The Princess Heir smiled a ghastly grin with her teeth bared against her walnut skin. "You know what these are for, right?" as she grasped an open manacle dangling from the wall.

"Some of my ancestors were inventive," she said. "A couple of them liked to tie prisoners to the walls with metal shackles and watch them burn with the power."

Ciardis began struggling against her captors. Dammit, she didn't want to fry!

"Alas," sighed the Princess Heir, "that fate is not for you—not today. I don't have time to get a weather mage here. Besides, I need you alive."

"Your friend, on the other hand, is of no use to me," she said while speaking to Ciardis. Seating herself in a chair, she called out, "Soundsoar! Get to it."

Ciardis turned in horror to watch Damias being chained to the wall. Though he struggled, he couldn't overpower his captors.

Then Lord SoundSoar stepped forward with death in his eyes.

Marissa said, "He does so enjoy this part."

Soundsoar raised his hand and clutched at the air just a few inches away from Damias throat. As he squeezed the empty air in front of Damias's face, Damias began to gasp for air, his face turning blue from lack of oxygen, and he kicked and twisted his body in desperation.

Just like the Grand Vizier.

"Stop it," screamed Ciardis. "You're killing him." She struggled with the two men holding her, finally twisting around enough to grab the knife from her back. She gutted one of the men immediately, but the other guard—an assassin, she was sure—disarmed her and punched her twice in the face.

She collapsed to her knees.

The next time she looked up, Damias was still struggling, his eyes rolling back in his head. Soundsoar was *enjoying* it. He had a sick, almost sexual, grin on his face.

Ciardis vomited. She wasn't quite sure if it was because she had a concussion or if she were just overwhelmed with the depravity.

Soon Damias went silent, his body slack and his head slumped.

Soundsoar sighed with contentment. Ciardis had never hated anyone so much.

The Princess Heir turned to Ciardis. "Now, my dear, it is your turn." With a snap of her fingers, she commanded the guard, "Bring her to me."

The guard forced Ciardis to her knees before the seated woman, and she stared up into the madwoman's eyes.

"What do you want from me?" Ciardis asked as the guard stood behind her holding her firmly on her knees.

Marissa cooed to Ciardis, "Your power, my dear, as I said before. I want it to be mine. It's the least you can do after ruining my plans."

She continued with a sadistic smile, "Don't worry. I'll be gentle. It would be bad of me to damage my only chance to drain the power of an enhancer companion."

As soon as the Princess Heir put her hands on either side of Ciardis's head, she felt the drain of magic begin.

A patron's pull was usually like the gentle tug of a friend's hand on a warm spring day; this felt like her brain was being scraped out of her head inch by inch.

She couldn't scream; she couldn't speak. She retreated into her magical core, huddled against the pain and force of the Princess Heir's power.

And then she heard a voice. "Ciardis?"

"Sebastian," she called out in relief and anguish. "Your aunt is crazy! Help us!"

"Where?" There was a pause. "Never mind—just hold on."

Ciardis pulled back further into the core, her presence dimming, and then all but disappearing.

"I said hold on!"

"I *am* holding on, you inconsiderate brat," she said.

He chuckled. "That's more like it. But no, I meant to hold on to something physical. It's about to get windy."

Bracing herself for the pain and whatever it was Sebastian was about to do, Ciardis opened her eyes and lunged for the princess's chair in a moment of desperation. She clutched the Princess Heir's legs as if her life depended on it.

And then the storm came. The top of the needle broke off and suddenly the entire room was open to the elements. An Ansari man with the wingspan of a god and the attire of the Gardis dropped into the room from the sky. In his arms he carried a young prince. The Ansari set Sebastian down behind a second guard, and he took in the situation.

"Aunt Marissa," Sebastian said coldly. "You missed my coronation festivities."

The woman stood up from her chair and kicked Ciardis's pale form back. "Well you know how my schedule is, dear nephew."

There were now two assassin guards—plus two evil Mages, versus her, Sebastian, and two Ansari Gardis.

Deciding this was a fair time to comment, Ciardis said, "I told you to bring help, Sebastian, not barge in here prepared to die."

Then the battle began. Lord Soundsoar called in high winds from the sky. The winds were strong enough to smash the Ansari Gardis against the far wall, if they hadn't been ready for his attack. They shielded against Soundsoar's gale winds and one of the Ansari Gardis pulled out of his pocket a glass ball with clear crystals inside. The clear crystals looked like shards—shards of crushed glass. It took a moment for her to realize the implications, but when she did, Ciardis dropped her body fully to the floor.

The Ansari Gardis tossed the ball to the floor, causing it to break and glass to fly into the air. As the glass fell back to the ground, a fierce wind came in through the roof. The wind formed a terrifying funnel, scooping up the glass and turning the deadly winds to the side of the room which held the Princess Heir, the assassin guards, Soundsoar and unfortunately – Ciardis.

"Hey, man—I'm over here, too!" she shouted at the Ansari Gardis from the ground, her head buried in her arms. He didn't acknowledge her. The glass gale went straight down the throats of Soundsoar and the first assassin. They collapsed, coughing bright globs of blood onto their vestments. Their lungs had ruptured from the internal assault. It looked like both were dead.

Deciding she didn't want to die on the floor, Ciardis crawled across the bodies and grabbed the dagger from Soundsoar's sheath. She was tempted to spit on him, but decided she'd do it later.

Looking up, it was clear to Ciardis that even with the deaths of Soundsoar and the assassin, her rescuers were losing the battle. The other assassin had decapitated Sebastian's second guard, and the Princess Heir was draining the mage powers of everyone in the room.

It was up to her to change the tide of battle. She knew she had only seconds while the Princess Heir's concentration was occupied. She grabbed her knife and prepared to rush her.

And then the Princess Heir stopped. Without warning, the knife was snatched away from Ciardis, leaving a deep gash on her wrist.

Soundsoar had grabbed it. He couldn't use it because he couldn't get up off the floor from where he lay in a dark pool of blood. In a fit of anger, Ciardis kicked his chest with enough force that his lungs continued their downward spiral; he died instantaneously.

The distraction gave the Ansari guard enough time to hit the Princess Heir with a wave of air that forced her into the wall, snapping her neck in the process. Her limp body dropped to the floor with a *thud*, as did her last remaining guard.

He was dead when Ciardis approached him.

Silently, the Ansari Gardis who introduced himself as Michael checked the bodies in the room. He summoned the Gardis next to Ciardis. Sebastian was huddled against a wall, shivering. Soon other guards flowed into the room. They prepared to remove Damias's body and Ciardis moved forward with them to silently walk beside her tutorials instructor as they carried his body from the room.

CHAPTER TWENTY

She mourned Damias as best she could after filling out report after report on the tower incident for both the Companions' Guild and the Imperial Court. Days later she had a very unsettling conversation with the general. It started with the general asking how many children she was planning to bear, and had abruptly ended with him asking her how soon she planned to start. Speechless, Ciardis excused herself and raced to her room, suddenly anxious to find Sebastian. She donned the red dress she had planned to wear to that afternoon's dance and a black cloak to conceal the gown. She couldn't care less what Serena thought at the moment.

Racing uphill to the carriage, she almost asked the driver to take her to the Imperial Palace, but she knew there was no way she'd get through the gates—not by herself and not without an invitation, so she swallowed the request and turned back. Cursing under her breath, she raced back down the slope to the gardens of the Companions' Guild through the main hall and down the slope. Soon she reached down and activated the Aether anklet with a touch of her fingertips. For a minute, all was blurry, and then she was in the other Aether realm.

She'd been picturing the city of Sandrin, and so the bracelet had taken her there—or, at least, it had taken her to the surrounding area. The city cliffs rose high above her and the water lapped gently while she strode on the beach. *Great. Now what?*

Deciding that she should at least try to contact Sebastian mind-to-mind, she tapped into her mage core to search for any sign of another mage nearby. There was no one, but out of the corner of her eye she suddenly saw several brilliant flashes of gold.

The gold glowed on the edges of her vision. It was in the soft lap of the waves, shimmering in the tiny grains of sand, and it was etched like an elegant filigree along the cliffs. Hesitantly, she reached out to touch the gold in the cliffs, thrumming the magic, calling its name.

Protect, guard, save, was the feeling the gold magic sent to her. Save what, though?

She reached out again with her gift, this time giving it her power. It was instinctual to her, this desire to enhance the magical protections that lay before her. The filigree, the grains of sand, the gold-laced waves—all were a part of the protection spells laid across the land of Algardis.

She thrummed some more.

"What are you doing?" demanded an exasperated voice from behind her.

Smiling, she turned around. "So it *was* you. I recognized the feel of your magic and the power of the Land Wight. I knew the spells could have only been done by you. You laid all these protections."

Sebastian frowned at her before answering uncomfortably, "No, I inherited these protection spells, and then I strengthened them." He shrugged as he looked up at the cliffs. "How'd you know it was me?"

This time, she shrugged. "It felt like you."

"Great. Well then, if you're done, I'll be leaving."

"Wait! Wait! I'm sorry! I never meant to insult you. What do I have to do to make this right?"

"You got what you wanted. Isn't that enough?" he said coldly.

"I have patrons and power and pretty dresses—everything I ever wanted while I was in Vaneis. Everything I ever dreamed of is in my grasp. But I need a friend. I see that now. None of those court fops or companions are my friends—well, except for one. But I need one more."

He stared at her and kicked up a bit of sand with his shiny black boot. Glancing up at the sky and then back down at her, he sighed and said, "So could I." With a deep bow, he asked, "Milady, would you care to accompany me to the Afternoon Ball?"

She curtsied and replied, "I would be delighted."

He grasped her hands, grinning, while reaching within himself to activate the spell that would take them away from the Aether. With a mischievous smile, she said, "No, let me. I think this bracelet has a little power left in it."

With a swirl of magic, they were transported to the beach just below the Companions' Guild courtyard. Music drifted down the Cliffside to the beach from the orchestra above.

Ciardis took off her dark cloak and unpinned her hair. Impishly, she asked, "Would you care for a dance, milord?"

He blushed a deep crimson. The blush ran all the way down to the collar of his white shirt. The dress looked beautiful on her, she knew; the red set off her dark skin and her chestnut curls, which fell seductively down her back.

As he stepped forward across the sand to accept her invitation, Ciardis couldn't help but think he was accepting more than an invitation to dance.